WHITEOUT CONDITIONS

A NOVEL BY

TARIQ SHAH

Two Dollar Radio
Books too loud to Ignore

Two Dollar Radio
Books too loud to Ignore

WHO WE ARE TWO DOLLAR RADIO is a family-run outfit dedicated to reaffirming the cultural and artistic spirit of the publishing industry. We aim to do this by presenting bold works of literary merit, each book, individually and collectively, providing a sonic progression that we believe to be too loud to ignore.

TwoDollarRadio.com

Proudly based in
Columbus
OHIO

@TwoDollarRadio
@TwoDollarRadio
/TwoDollarRadio

Love the
PLANET?
So do we.

Printed on Rolland Enviro.
This paper contains 100% post-consumer fiber, is manufactured using renewable energy - Biogas and processed chlorine free.

100%   **PCF**   BIO GAS *ENERGY*   PERMANENT

Printed in Canada

RECOMMENDED LOCATIONS FOR READING *WHITEOUT CONDITIONS*: Upon a Greyhound bound for Rockford by midnight, within view of a bare forest, a hospital, or pretty much anywhere because books are portable and the perfect technology!

AUTHOR PHOTO→
Craig Durante

COVER ARTWORK→
Two Dollar Radio

> . . . *The dark adjusts*
> *itself, settles its wings inside you. The shadows that*
> *strut the dark*
> *open and fold like hope, a paper fan, violence*
> *in its pitch and fall, like waves—above them, the usual*
> *seabirds, their presumable*
> *indifference to chance, its*
> *blond convergences . . . As when telling cruelty apart*
> *from chivalry can come to seem irrelevant, or not anymore*
> *the main point . . .*
>
> —Carl Phillips

> *you won't get far by yourself.*
> *it's dark out there.*
> *there's a long way to go.*
> *the dog knows.*
>
> —Robert Creeley

WHITEOUT CONDITIONS

I

With the last of my loved ones now long dead, I find funerals kind of fun. Difficult to pinpoint what it is. I'm drawn to them. Call it an article of faith. They aren't what they used to be. And I am not my old self.

I'm thinking of the deep boom and hush after the pastor shuts his thick tome of hymns, and the heavy groans of the pews when everyone kneels.

What comes to mind are the high school boneheads loafing around the holy water stoup, too rad to grieve, or who never learned how, never learned that it is learned, like formal dinner etiquette, or gallantry in the face of certain peril.

It's the secret stoner altar boy glad to swing his censer, the blown-apart family uniting for a minute to ridicule the reverend's lopsided toupee. The great uncle with trouble reading in the filmy pulpit daylight, his index finger trembling.

Or when I drift off during an old man's eulogy, only to get clocked in the forehead with a truth bolt changing my vision of retired Honda dealers forever. *At a certain point the mileage accrued by hearts, like any muscle car, is just too fantastic.*

Once it was the apoplectic rage of a niece pacing the narthex, denied the chance to damn her uncle to hell, tell him she loved him.

Sometimes it's the waterworks, other times, the hearse.

It was the pious haste with which Muslim grievers dug the grave, buried the doctor, how that left everyone in a swarm, a bit head-spun, and forgetful the dead's dead.

The wholehearted embraces given me by Evangelists to whom I didn't speak at all, the fervent strangers touched I'm there, who cared I'd come, each hug verging on a submission hold, and it's the bright secret that won't quit tap-dancing behind my benign expression that I keep from them, that ensures their enthusiasm and sincerity are squandered on me.

Or a jogger, sometimes there will be a jogger, who will gawk like a rubbernecker, or just keep jogging, maybe go a little faster.

Seeing my buddies in suits for the first time, a grandmother past remembering why she's there. Sometimes it's as simple as a song of tribute sung by someone who can't sing at all. You see people for who they are, and they don't mind being seen, and it's lovely in a way, that unabashed flawed-ness in the face of such heavy exposure, perhaps never to happen again.

All of which would likely be overlooked were I choked up by the stiff in the coffin.

It's everyone wondering what I am doing there. It's all the suspicious looks—*why aren't you sad like us?* How they all ping off me.

Shadowing Death. Handling death like a snake charmer fishing cobras from his wicker basket, wholly impervious to fang and by now safely immune to its venom. And how sometimes, it's the other way around.

Funerals are kind of fun, yes. I've cultivated a taste. It's become a kind of social pursuit. It was a kink, of a kind.

But now Ray. I see his face, the one in the photograph the reporter in the field held up to the camera, with its fresh acne, and his right cheek's dimple deeper than I remember, and him already taller than his mother, and I'm having trouble sustaining a positive mental attitude. Now, a python's double-jointed jaws, Death opens wide. But, what do I know about such creatures?

*

I consider putting all of this to big old Hank, who, after sucking down his third screwdriver beside me on the plane, gets talkative, wonders why I'm flying, what with the weather—Chicago had a heavy white Christmas chased by a short thaw, but the Channel 9 weather guy predicts a monster on the horizon. I say, "funeral," as though it were a destination wedding.

He's a day trader on the futures market. Manicured nails, plump baby face, silver cufflinks. He would think I'm horsing around, some sort of wise guy, and eventually expect a rational explanation, request a change of seats. But I'm coming clean.

"Ever play with matches as a kid?" I ask.

He clears his throat and nods, uncertain, as a pocket of choppy weather jostles the cabin, making Hank spill half his drink all over his nifty polka dot tie. After glancing down the aisle, he sucks the alcohol directly from the raw blue silk.

I pretend not to notice. Outside the window, Illinois' patchwork of snow-dusted farmland scrolls underneath us, the color of month-old bread. The freeways and interstates carving colossal esoteric runes into it. The tiny black trees that suture it all together.

"Vince and I," I say, "we used to slick our arms in Aqua Net and light ourselves on fire. Our new rippling blue sleeves blowing our minds. Funerals are like that now. Only everyone else is burning for real, and I'm completely fine." I down the dregs of my coffee. "You ever do that?"

Hank buckles his safety belt, says he can't stand landings, so I drop it. All this turbulence is getting to me, too.

*

I'm back home, braving O'Hare's crowds—the holidays are through but concourse K is still a nightmarish glut of holly jolly backwash—slowpoke vacationers and duty-free shopaholics, Bing Crosby, and on-sale candy cane pyramid displays that all hound me faster for the exits.

It's been a few years since I last saw Vince, who is on his way to get me out of here. We are off to Big Bend, to bury what's left of his little cousin—Ray.

I heard about it on the morning news. I caught the tail end of the broadcast. The young face on the screen seemed an organic extension of something startling in its familiarity to me. The sensational nature of the incident pushed the story into wider media markets, I think. All the way to the East Coast.

So I gave Vince a call. I said I would come out. Give a show of support. Though I could have done less, I said it was the least I could do. Vince and his family sort of took me in after my own family's disintegration.

The last time I saw Ray, I think, he was eight and I had just finished school. It was Vince's birthday, middle autumn some-time. We cooked out. I remember Vince giving Ray his first taste of liquor, a swig from his Solo cup of Captain Morgan-and-whatever. Then spending the afternoon with them, shooting hoops in the drive, a few old folks in lawn chairs giving color commentary.

I remember watching Ray take that sip and Vince asking him, "How you like the taste of that?"

Ray made this sour face and said, "Beer's better." All the old folks ate that right up.

*

Slinking out past the baggage carousels, I have a post-flight cigarette that hits me so hard I swoon and gag like a rookie. But the parking garage fumes are a pleasant surprise. There is something I find nostalgic in the odor—all maple syrup and gasoline and the exhaust of a couple hundred idling taxicabs.

It's been around five years since I've been back, and yet the puddles of slush by the wall where smokers shelter from the cruel gusts seem pitiless as ever, black and bottomless, an inky soup. I've missed even them.

Here the sky yawns white all day, then rips your head off like afterburners once the sun falls off the horizon. But when the cold comes, it comes like a dream, lugging the dark in a big black sack. And my body readjusts to the old song it knows by heart.

Planes arrive and depart. I know Vince's circling around here somewhere, eyes peeled for someone I barely resemble now. I forget the kind of car he drives. It's one of those big dependable American makes, four doors and the type of interior that's not the leather option. The sort of car they don't really make anymore, built with a once-fine quality and craftsmanship that has long since fallen out of practice. One of those made-up names that seems real.

But who knows what state it's in. I smear out the smoke and wait on the outer traffic island for some kind of sign of him.

*

My dad never drank. That lent him a certain polish that Ruby, the other woman, must have found magnetic. He was always the designated driver, the voice of reason drumming sense into whomever was first to get rowdy at dinner parties, the one who really had no patience for Mom's drunk juggling, and who more than anything, seemed to love to be the one to carry her up to bed.

I, on the other hand, loved it when she drunk-juggled. She always started off small. We'd be in the kitchen getting dinner ready, Dad either home or on his way.

"Hey, Ant, check this out," she'd say—never when I was looking at her—and when I did, she'd have a couple fingerling potatoes going with one hand, while the other swirled a cast iron pan of chopped onions.

I would applaud her, then resume whatever homework, finger painting, or action figure brawl I'd been absorbed with.

A little bit later I would hear, "Uh oh!"

I'd look up again, and there'd be red and green bell peppers vaulting into the air. And then the salt shaker, a few tablespoons. By her third glass of merlot she'd be on to the chef's knife, the cleaver, three or four champagne flutes.

One time, instead of the performance, I watched her face. Despite all that deadly hardware being airborne, her expression wasn't one of deep focus, but simple amusement. She was only interested in my wonder, beholding this marvelous act, this peculiar talent of hers.

When she caught me looking at her, she winked. Then, calmly, she closed her eyes. Mom kept the spectacle going until a flute hit the floor, exploded, and we both laughed our heads off.

She was gifted with the hands of a surgeon. They never trembled, or fumbled, or missed, even in the numbing winter mornings and dark. Her hands were steady, clever instruments, and worked with an agile precision that I found beautiful to watch.

For a long time I believed her touch cured the migraines I would get as a boy. Her palms were dry and cool, soft as calfskin, and seemed to draw the pulse from its place behind my eyes. But the relief came from some other place, I think now.

She kept her nails plain, and whenever the Avon lady encouraged her to paint them, or worse, hinder them with Lee Press Ons, Mom would get this crooked kind of look and see her to the door.

She claimed she could do chainsaws, had juggled them before, but we only ever had the one.

After the divorce, her weird charm grew brittle. Over time, she became the sober, pragmatic one. What home had become eventually became normal, until high school started. Everything changes for everybody, but for us especially, since the doctors felt a lump in her left breast. Then a mass at the base of her spine. This was right around homecoming, and Dad, who had at least kind of still been around, began to venture further out to the periphery of our lives until he was more absent than present, more answering machine than man.

But she still drunk-juggled from time to time, around the holidays, or the date of their anniversary. I still clapped like hell. She died that fall, just before Thanksgiving. The funeral was sober, pragmatic.

I have no idea whether Ruby drinks, or whether it was his sobriety she found attractive, or just the veneer it cast—either way, he must have preferred her figure to Mom's wildness. And I don't hope he is dead but I act according to that assumption. When I find myself low on that, I simply wish it.

The way it goes. I don't pull sour faces anymore—I figure dead or alive, he's gone for good. That's pretty reliable. It does the trick. Still—beer is better.

*

Vince lays on the horn when he sees me. I heave my bag into the trunk and hop in like we've done this a hundred times.

"Your hair is long," I tell him. It's past his collar, though it's also receding.

"Need to get a cut soon. Caroline likes it."

"So the lady next to me at the airport bar got bombed and would not stop pushing her dopey son's deep funk band on me. Deep funk or free funk, I can't remember. He goes to JUCO. He's the next Ornette Coleman, so that's something. No, it was liquid funk, but what that is I do not know. Playing a lunchtime set at the Cubby Bear tonight or tomorrow. Gonna be 'a real toe-tapper,' apparently."

Vince doesn't even smile. "Things are good with you, then."

I shrug—at him, and at everything I could tell him, at all I could say in response, my hoard of thoughts and tidings and urges that want a voice, a breath. I keep them stashed. "Feels nice, riding in this behemoth again. How's things with you?"

He twists around to scope out a gap in the traffic to merge into. "We're managing," he says.

The windshield has a hairline fracture knifing slowly toward the center of the pane, the one-knob-missing radio doesn't seem to get anything but AM, and I'm up to my ankles in wadded Taco Bell trash, which I bury my feet in, searching for the floor.

"Could you not stomp all over my stuff, please? I need all that for work and if I give back a bunch of broke equipment to my boss…"

I hold up a plug head. "What, this?"

"That cable's for the reciprocating saw. It's not mine. Don't monkey with it."

"Maybe you shouldn't leave it tangled up on the floor under blankets of garbage."

"It was fine how I had it before you started getting your muddy, salty shoes all over everything."

"Here, I'll coil it up." I root through the fountain cups and wrappers to the orange cord beneath it all and begin looping it.

"Eh, don't worry about it," he says. "They had a piano guy playing at the mall this year. Some Christmas thing. Thought of you for a second."

"Flattered."

Vince smirks. "Beneath you, forgot."

"How are *you*, other than *man*aging? What's Caroline up to these days?"

"She and the kids are in Disney World right now. That was their Christmas gift—an arm and a leg of their old man's. They're staying outside the park though, at some high school friend of Caroline's with a place in Kissimmee. Flying back sometime Sunday."

"They must be a handful."

"She made me zap my balls last month. Two's just shy of too much for us."

"Wendy was big on starting a family. Saw herself having five, six. A great big litter. Red flag right there, if there ever was one."

Vince nods. "Who's Wendy now?"

I wave away the question. "Ah, just a girl. You know. Came and went."

Vince cuts in front of a van, into hectic traffic, his car spewing bluish exhaust behind us like a sad magician's trick.

I just shrug.

The route gains familiarity, despite my time away. A few ancient billboards still stand, though they are largely dilapidated beyond recognition—just a smoky eye, half a restaurant logo ripping in the wind, the unnerving command *Hurry!*—being all that's left of them. I struggle to find something to fill the vacuum of silence between us.

"Know any good songs?"

He shakes his head, and we're quiet again.

As the road meanders west, forest thins into strip mall, and thick, crooked black cracks start riddling the road home.

"You missed our turn," I tell him.

"No, I didn't."

"You did. Our exit was back there. We need to go north on 94."

"We're taking a quick field trip. Have to run an errand."

"Traffic's gonna hit any minute."

"Just pipe down, will you? Giving me a headache."

He pulls up to a drab McMansion with a high stone archway and a roller hockey net knocked over in the yard. There's a pair of dark-tipped steer horns mounted in leatherette above a big glass door with a bright brass knob.

"Stay here," Vince says, getting out. From the rearview I see him pop the trunk, hear the heavy equipment—more power tools, most likely—hit the ground. The lid thuds shut, making the car bounce a little bit. Then it's even quieter than before.

I crane my neck to look around: not a single soul, no one around. Two minutes become five. I light a cigarette and get out to stretch my legs and escape the car's reek of old fries and strawberry air freshener. Five minutes become ten and I stroll to the end of the driveway, where I can see, just beyond the T-intersection that we turned into, a street sign that reads "Evergreen Lane," so bent it points to the pothole beneath it.

I look back at the house: not a creature stirring. I'm halfway down the block before I realize it, my feet like those of an old horse returning to stable.

I knew it was probably a lousy idea, going back to my old house. Until the idea came into my head, I hadn't thought about my old place at all. It was a corny idea. I had no idea what to expect it to do. It was an ugly house, just like all the houses surrounding it. It was drafty in the winter and a sweat lodge in the summer. It slouched on one side, drooped, as if it had once suffered a stroke. Barely any backyard, no real front lawn. Hard water, orange water from the taps, unless you plunked a 25-pound block of salt in the softener a couple times a month. A basement that flooded every year when the pipes froze and burst. An attic overrun with yellow jackets. And the only thing shabbier than the aesthetics were the memories I still had of living there. But anyway, when would I be back here again?

I take a right at the corner, go up Evergreen Lane, even though I know Evergreen Lane, and Evergreen Lane never looked much at all like this. Though the land is the same—a soft rise just before the plummet that leads to the river and the concrete bridge leaping it that transforms into bland, interstate high-way—almost everything on top of it has changed. My feet keep going. I'm losing light, but feel it's close. I search the stores and little homes for their numbers. I walk past an unlit credit union, a bargain store with guitars hung in the windows, and I worry I might have passed it, or forgotten the way, but that's impossible. I go by a dialysis center, a seafood place, some kids trudging home with their sleds. I knew this place backward and forward.

Soon, there is a bowling alley, its sign of neon red pins already searing through the new evening dark. I slow to a stop. I'm standing in the parking lot of Holy Roller Lanes & Arcade. Looking around me, I see, one street over behind a break in some spindly, wind-bothered trees, the crooked house of an old neighbor, whose face resists my mind's conjuring. Someone I didn't like, or didn't really know, or who was more a friend of Mom's than of mine.

It dawns on me then—I'm standing in my living room.

Behind me, a car horn sounds, and there's Vince, watching me, smoking out the window. "They made your street a cul-de-sac. Guess your old man sold the place when the alley opened up. Had to make room."

"What was the hold up back at that house?"

"Needed to return some gear, borrow some good shoes." He shrugs. Classic Vince, really, but still.

"Oh, a real emergency then."

He snorts, gestures at the empty lot. "And this? Some kind of five-alarm fire?"

An ambulance screams by, making us dizzying blue and red until that recedes as the sound goes flat. I kick a hunk of asphalt into the middle of the lot.

"Expect the world to stand still for you? You need a hug?"

"Ah," I say, "to hell with it."

I bite my lip. One pain muffles another, and who cares. Then with a quick little tick, we're the off yellow of the street lamp overhead. For that moment, we're lit up, then we keep going.

Once we're into a bit of open road, I say, "How'd that hand happen?"

Vince holds it up like he's surprised to find it braced and bandaged. "Work accident. Hammered myself," he says. "Stupid of me. There was a babe walking by. It's not bad. Tingles more than anything."

"You should get your balls zapped again. Maybe they didn't finish the job."

He coughs. "That was a joint decision. Me and Caroline are fine." Vince adds, "It's Marcy and Dan in rough shape…"

He fingers around in the change holder for his pack of Pall Malls. When he finds them he lights up, steering with his knee. We drift from the left lane to old tawdry snow—a running scab of gray snot where the road's shoulder was. He rolls down the window. Cold air gushes in. The guy behind us beeps and Vince corrects course. I light one too.

He shouts over the roar, "They couldn't identify the body. So I did."

"How'd he look?"

"How you *think* he looked?"

"It was just a question, okay?"

"He looked like everything else Bullets ever got at."

It's so easy for me to forget things about people I used to know. Just hearing that name.

I remember trying to teach Bullets tricks when he was a pup. Shake hands, I'd command, tapping his outsized paw. I got bit one day doing that. Just a nip, but that's when lessons ended, maybe a month before I moved away.

He was our friendly neighborhood dirtbag pervert Gavin Kwasneski's dog. Even as a kid, Gavin was pretty foul, prone to peeping, cornering girls, lifting skirts, that kind of thing, but that was all one heard about back then. Still, the lore gave us all the creeps and whenever something new happened, we would look askance at him right before looking the other way, preferring thoughts less vile. Years passed.

One afternoon he knocked on my door. He began explaining to me the sex violations that landed him nine months in Joliet Correctional, from which he was freshly released—rehabilitated, a new man, he claimed, with a very off-putting kindness in his voice.

I never knew any of the people Gavin hurt, and aside from these encounters he barely registered in my or Vince's life at all. He was just one of those things people bury as well as they can. Because that works for a while. One day though, as you're going about your business, you end up tripping on a tiny little itty-bitty rock in the ground, the rock turns out to be a bone, and you can't help it—you start digging.

Gavin had a puppy with him. He gathered it up in his arms.

"This is my new doggy," he said, and held out a vanilla-white pup, its nose pink as a piglet's.

"Hi, doggy."

I remember the pup gave a yawn. Gavin dropped him; it hit the ground hard. Then they shuffled over to the next house.

*

"They're shutting down the high school," Vince says. He feeds his cigarette through the window slit but it flies back in, onto the backseat.

"Nice. I loved snow days."

"Not for the weather—for the mourning, you dummy. They're having some sort of memorial for him on Monday."

Vince goes to swat out the burning filter with his free hand but he can't reach. We swerve hard this time.

"Not even two feet of snow on the ground," he says, "and it's like twenty out. They won't even think about closing unless it's below zero."

I tell him to just focus on not killing us. Keep a window cracked.

*

I love that funeral parlors are like fake living rooms. How they appear to be equal parts resort hotel lobby and sitcom set for the bereaved. The knockoff Turners and Titians proudly hung in the foyer, the bowl of Starlight Mints, the chandelier around which the staircase dovetails. The ashtrays, all at the ready, inside every desk and coffee table drawer. The raw wood aroma you get opening up the cabinets, of sawdust; the unvacuumed carpeting strangers trample with their dress shoes on, the film of spilt coffee burning on the gummy hotplate.

I love that it could almost be someone's home, nondescript save the marquee in the drive, the brass plaque beside the doorbell. They try so hard, and yet the further one pokes around, the more abnormal it becomes—the bare cupboards, hollow clocks, empty closets, the absence of cohesion a family brings to a household, with their framed photos, dog-eared *Sports Illustrated* issues, their toothbrush cups by the sink and the general disorder of socks, muddy sneakers, dishes, junk mail that enlivens the places we inhabit. That there are no watercolor paintings, softball schedules, shopping lists, bright silly magnets—nothing is ever stuck to the door of the fridge.

The whole show—the bouquets and black-out drapes, the living room chapels, the organs droning out dirges to drum-machine beats, the discount casket coupons thumbtacked by the phone, padlocked basement door—none of it is morbid, to me, anymore.

I love the hearse, the motorcade following behind it, and the little paper tickets you put in the windshield, and running red lights, headlights on in the daytime. The little plastic hooks by which the living hang potted flowers beside the graves, like lanterns. I love the giant register everyone must sign. I love the bad lemon tea on offer, the stale cookies in their plastic tray, how there's never milk, only powdered sugar-free creamer. I love that it's all a terrible party thrown midday, midweek, at a house with never enough parking, nothing at all to do, that no one can stand to be in for more than an hour. Except me.

*

The problem was little Ray had Dan's .22 revolver pointed right up his own nose when Vince and I got back from our emergency beer run. He was in the TV room, watching Bert and Ernie, just as he'd been when we left ten minutes before. He beamed our way as we walked in and kicked off our shoes.

"Hi, Vin. Hey, Ant," Ray said, waving hello with the pistol.

Vince froze. "Where the hell you get that? Put that down."

Ray hugged the gun to his chest.

"That is not a toy, leave it be. I got a surprise for you."

"A *surprise?*" He jumped for joy.

"Ray, *stop*. Listen now: please place that gun on the carpet—*nicely*. Right now."

"Why?"

"Just do it, please."

Ray took a tentative step toward us, then a step back, as he thought it over. "It's mine. *I* found it."

"Goddamn," said Vince, and he looked at me. I set down the bag of beer.

"Ray," I said, "what about a trade, yeah? You give me the gun, I'll give you—*these...*" I dangled the car keys before him. Ray pointed the handgun at me.

"Cars are better, bud. How about it?" I said, giving them a jingle.

"I'll even throw in this king-size Snickers," Vin said. "That seal the deal?"

Ray's attention reeled back to the TV, to Bert and Ernie counting sheep.

"*Ray*. The *gun...*" I said.

"Fine..."

And then the thing went off. Startled, Ray's hands went to his ears as he started crying and ran off to his room. Vince got the .22.

I started calling him "Ray the Gun" after that. Then that turned into just "Raygun." He was "Raymond" before all this, a dweeby little spazz born with coke-bottle glasses and an overbite.

Vince likes to dispute this fact. He claims we both came up with the nickname. If being in the same room as someone who thinks of something means you think up the thing too, then yes, Vince helped. But he knows the truth.

I wasn't close to Ray like Vince was. But I did contribute.

Ray loved it. It made him feel tough and dangerous. And then you have all the variations: Death Ray, Gay Run, Stun Gunner, and so on.

I suppose I felt good about making him feel cool like that. A nickname lends personality to the bearer, indicates a reputation, prior achievements of note, that there are people on your side—a tribe, however dwindling. Says, *I have done things, I have friends.* But all the nicknames turned out pretty useless in the end.

*

As Vince drives, I say, "Ray the Gun. Remember *that* day?"

He glances my way. "Dan broke a broom handle on me that night, that's what I remember."

"Dan's the one to blame—you keep a loaded handgun in a shoebox under the bed with kids in the house, you're asking for it. He ought to know better. Under the bed's the first place they look."

"You should have let me handle it."

"Like you're some hostage negotiator. It was not the smartest tactic in the world—fine. Did anyone get shot?"

He frowns at the window, changes lanes again.

"What use is there arguing about it anyway? Look where we are now," I say.

He lets out a long, slow breath. "I remember us posting up on the couch after all that, just in time to catch The Undertaker tombstone Mr. Perfect. Not missing a beat."

"No use letting all that beer get warm…" I say.

"Marcy kicked both Ray's *and* Dan's asses that night, actually."

"And you beat mine. Nearly broke my nose. Don't think I forgot."

Vince wags his head. "Raygun. Damn…"

Remembering the bullet hole, like a shark's vacant eye staring at me, lodged in the wall just inches wide of my left ear. The one and only slug ever shot off in my presence, that for the longest time I was convinced had my name on it. But the world had different plans for me, didn't it. I put on my everything's-fine grin. The world is screaming past my shoulder in a humming blur of frozen sludge and rail.

*

And then there was later that summer, the summer I left, and the heat wave that claimed over 200 lives across the county. The power grid couldn't handle the strain and failed on the second night; everyone was plunged in a smothering dark that left everything tacky, damp, and smudged. All of us slightly addlebrained and reluctant to get the mail.

Leaving the front and back doors open only invited breezes that came in and swept through the house like the trapped air of a hot parked car. Playing the piano left it slippery and glistening with so much sweat I worried it would somehow warp the action on the keys. I didn't play for days.

Vince was turning a little bitter, a little weird about me leaving, but we still hung out pretty much every day, drinking Schlitz or clowning around or griping about not having money, or planning Vince's wedding, or having nothing to do at all, really. That summer sucked, for everybody.

We were all fooling around out in back, playing with the hose, trying to get a water war started against some of the neighborhood gang. The afternoon humidity made everyone too slow to choose sides, set ground rules, so it never really materialized. We mostly ended up sprawled on the porch, telling each other what we wished we had to eat—even though the fridge was probably full of stuff, it never looked good to us and even if that were not the case, the heat left us with little motivation to do much but moan and groan.

I wished for a foot-long barbecue beef and cheese submarine sandwich, butter garlic fries from the Lemon Tree diner up the road, a gallon of raspberry iced tea. Vince wished for thick wedges of cold pizza, a strong bloody Mary.

All Ray wished he had was popsicles, so we took a walk down to Bad's General Store because they sold bomb pops. We were too lazy to find our shoes, so we just cut through spiky yellowed lawns and searing back lots in bare feet and towels 'round our swim trunks. Rudy Tomczak wouldn't care about selling to shoeless kids on a burning day. We bought the last box.

We passed by Gavin's on the way back, and there was Bullets tied up in the sun. His leash was looped in the tires of Gavin's pickup parked in the bed of gravel outside his house.

The dog was pinned in that punishing midday blast of light and couldn't get to the Tupperware bowl of old gross water that a couple pill bugs thought was a swimming pool. He was mangy and hyperventilating, letting the green flies roaming his belly and face have their way.

Ray started wandering over, wanting to get a better look. Ray was curious. He maybe thought Bullets was already a goner and wanted to check it out. We trailed him, brushing stones and twigs off of our heels, while the alien frequency of the cicadas droning rose and fell and made the stillness that followed somehow deeper and sort of blue to me.

Ray, shielding his eyes from the sunlight shafting through those elms, walked over. When Bullets growled, it was more like a purr of annoyance, seeing as he didn't bother to move.

Nearing up until he was about within arm's reach, Ray offered Bullets a lick of his orange popsicle. Like it was a microphone, he pointed it toward Bullets' slack mouth, grew closer until the cold blunt nose of it landed on the dog's tongue. I neared too, as Ray gently ran it back and forth like he was applying chapstick, letting it melt until Bullets tasted it, smacked his lips, and suddenly snapped to life and began lapping at it desperately.

Vince and I watched for a while as Bullets licked down Ray's bomb pop and even took the popsicle stick. Ray rubbed his belly, shooed the flies. *Well*, I thought, *Ray made a pal today.*

Then Vince went back to the road to smoke in the shade there.

"Yo," I said, tapping Ray's bony shoulder, "time to go."

"He'll fry."

"We're gonna get in trouble. Come on."

Ray frowned. "Would *you* wanna dry up like a worm in the road?"

"You're a little puke, Ray. I swear."

So, I get to freeing the stupid leash from the front tire it had gotten wound around when the dog must have tried hiding underneath the truck to escape the heat. The growl Bullets gave me was this gurgling in his throat. When he bared his teeth I clapped his mouth shut, held him by the muzzle, held it closed, and getting nose-to-snout, told him to be nice, I was helping him.

His growling unraveled as I shushed him and got him to chill out, but still, those blank eyes stared right into me, black as tar bubbles.

I said to Ray to give him some room, and unhooked the leash from Bullets' collar. Then I stood and let go. Bullets immediately galloped over to the water bowl and drank it dry, bugs and all. Then he started bouncing around, all giddy to be free, and leapt into the trash cans, knocked one over, and started disemboweling the garbage bags inside. What anything chained up too long would do.

We were walking out when we heard a voice go, "No, no, no no—you don't get to pet my dog. No one does. Only me."

And there came Gavin from around back, coming toward us, sweating awfully. Glistening streaks ran down his face, darkening his sleeveless shirt.

He knelt next to Ray and casually took him by the back of his neck, suddenly trying to be neighborly. "Now, you know this is private property. You know this is my dog," he said to Ray, shaking him lightly as he spoke. "You stay right there," he told Ray, and Ray obeyed. So did I.

I saw Vince approach, storm-faced, pick Gavin's hand up off Ray, and the whole world seemed to be reversing course at light speed. Vince was mad as a hornet, though Gavin had all kinds of weight on him, had all kinds of weird cunning. But Vince was spry. I almost couldn't watch.

And Gavin was a little shocked, watching his own hand get lifted away like a hot pan taken off a burner. But then his eyes grew keen, sort of bright with a weird joy he seemed to want kept secret. But I'd seen it before—we all had, at one time or another. With Gavin, you never knew what you were going to get—sadism or whimsy, Hook or Peter Pan. But, however he did choose to behave, it was always with a wild leer like that, trying to be hid, trying to be—harnessed.

Sometimes he was the alligator, too. Endless appetite, never too far.

Shrugging off that small invasion of his personal space, he gave a sharp whistle to grab the dog's attention, and after giving chase around the pickup a little while, managed to horse collar

Bullets. "Sit *down*," he commanded, and twisted the collar until the dog did as told. Just as quickly, Gavin's mind changed.

"*Move*, dumb dog," he said, and dragged Bullets back over to the truck, where he leashed him up again.

"Go easy…" Vince said. I could tell he spoke before thinking, the way he studied the dirt after the words left his mouth.

"I know, I know," he replied, sorry as a cardinal caught whoring, as he got up from his feet with a little whine, came over to us, and loped a long sweat-slick arm over Vince's shoulders. He began walking Vince around, talking to him. Casual as can be. Vince even let him do it at first, even when Gavin got real close and was whispering into Vince's ear.

"I love the dog, I do. Lot of responsibility in raising animals. You have to be firm…"

When Vince tried shrugging Gavin's arm off his shoulders, it became a headlock. The snare was triggered. Though he was much taller than all of us, his body was somehow both gangly and obese, like a tortoise in a too-big shell. Gavin worked him, smothering Vince in his armpit. Then he pivoted our way as Vince grunted, doing what he could to break it.

Gavin, playing the heel, mildly staring at me and Ray as Vince toiled under his flabby hold. Bullets, going into hiding under the pickup.

The seconds under that ugly gaze of his felt twisted and— outside of time, though it must have been only a moment, him watching us with this lazy, sleepy face, relishing our helplessness. Vince bucking madly then, throwing elbows into Gavin's doughy paunch. Ray starting to cry.

And then Gavin, grating his knuckles back and forth over Vince's scalp, muttering "keep fighting," bringing the whole thing to a hard boil until he finally quit it.

Vince, deep red and sucking air, turning away to smear off the sweat.

"We're just playing around, don't be scared," he said to Ray, this idiotic leer on his face. And as if it would prove his point, Gavin snatched at Ray's towel. There was a brief mock tug of war. He gleefully hammed it up a little, then released him, chuckled and scratched at his prickly throat.

"It's too hot," said Gavin, himself out of breath. "Parents, cops—you tell anyone, you'll be sorry…"

We all edged away until reaching the road. Gavin, bent double, hands on knees, watching us like a cross bull in the shade, before wandering around off to the backyard again, leaving the spilled trash all over the failing grass, where a couple Styrofoam plates cartwheeled from a weak breeze into the shrubs.

I took a final look behind me and there was Bullets, who barked some happy barks of goodbye before loping off to thrash around with the beach towel Ray'd left behind.

We walked most of the way back in a shaky, hyper, post-fight rush of disbelief. Vince smoked about ten cigarettes along the way. In a few days, there would show, along his neck, his clavicle, a swath of soft gray bruising, the imprint of Gavin's arm where he'd gripped him. He said not a word about it. Sometimes bruises are a badge.

The subdivision was a ghost town. As we passed the wood sign reading "Orchard Park" at the turn-in, it felt recently evacuated, which I took to mean the power had returned. Vince said nothing at all for a long time, until he noticed Ray had gone silent too.

"You good?" Vince asked.

Ray nodded. "Thanks, man," he whispered, and making his limp arm into a kind of swung weapon, playfully thwacked at Vince's side. Little dude code for *love you.*

"Next time it's your turn."

Ray studied the grass, sounded a nervous moan. He looked to me, his expression—*Is that so?* But I ignored it as though he wasn't there at all.

Still, he kept looking, his hands wringing themselves.

Then Vince scooped him up, put the boy's scrawny frame on his shoulders, gave him a lift back home, where we found the living room already growing comfortably cold.

*

After the news report concluded, I didn't call immediately. I've never been good with phones, and as the minutes went by, I became less certain what I saw was real. I stared at the gray television screen, convincing myself it had been, but my thoughts wouldn't stay still in my mind long enough to chart a logical course of action. I sat still like that until I felt about to explode. And when I rang Vince up it went down like this:

"May I speak to Vincent Von Jovic, please?"

"Who's calling."

I go, "Vince. Goddamnit, it's me, it's Ant. Antioch."

"*Ant.* Your voice finally dropped."

"I know. It's doing wonders for my love life. Sorry it's been so long. I've been busy. We're all busy, right?"

"How are you? Ahem, what can I, I mean—"

"I'm fine, I'm the same."

"Cool, yeah, good. Well this is probably about Ray then, I'm guessing."

"I'm calling about Ray, the Ray Gun, yeah. The news is saying all kinds of stuff. And I don't know, I just wanted to call. You and him were—you two were close, so—I mean, I was kind of friends with him too, you know?"

"I get you. Well I don't know, really. How to put this, I mean. There was an accident, night before last. We had an attack."

"What happened?"

"No one's really sure how it started or like, what exactly—or the play-by-play, know what I mean? Police are still investigating, so we'll probably never know. But Ray died. On the way to the hospital."

"Oh, god…"

"Kind of sucks."

"Oh, Christ. I'm sorry, Vince."

"Well… you should tell that to his mom and dad, maybe."

"Yeah, I'm calling them next. Think I have their number still. If I don't I'll let you know. How are you holding up though? I mean, like—"

"I'm maintaining. Funeral's in a couple days. I'm kind of just helping out the family with everything, you know."

"Well listen. I'd like to come out and attend. If that'd be all right with everyone."

"Must be expensive to fly out and all that hassle. It's nice of you, but don't feel obligated."

"If it's all the same to everyone, I can book a seat right now. Least I can do. Vince—sorry I've been so off the radar."

"Hey, man—things happen. Like you said, we're all busy…"

"Still, though. I wanted to say it."

"Wow, Ant. Listen to you. Sound so grown up. It's a two-way street though, I suppose. House full of kids is not conducive to the usual outreach efforts…"

"I'm sure they keep you and Caroline on your toes. So we're straight, right? It's all right I come?"

"Not gonna *bar you*, Ant. I'm heading up Saturday. I was gonna hit up a motel or something that night—service is Sunday. I'm working all day Saturday though, wouldn't get in until late. It's way up in Big Bend. Dan and Marcy got some relatives up there that don't travel so well, so... if you want a ride up with me, I can come get you."

"No way. That'd be great. We can catch up."

"If you like."

"I'll call you back later and let you know my details."

"It's a plan."

"Sorry again."

"Yeah, I heard you the first two times. You and me both. Sorry all around."

*

I was thrilled to have a little brother. Mom and I and Vince went on all kinds of shopping trips for stuff for the baby, and she'd get us prizes for being good on the way back home—sundaes, or tacos, sometimes comics, once a gerbil. I was eight or nine at the time.

She wanted a girl. A little baby girl to offset me and Vince. We were goons.

She was surrounded at all times by us savages always breaking stuff, wreaking havoc, profaning her home. She longed for a daughter who she could take to piano lessons and ballet class, to help her cook and bake cakes and sugar cookies, though we liked doing that with her too.

I wanted to be a big brother, to have someone who could test out sketchy sled runs. We could, I thought, gang up against Vince when he was being a dick, because he's a little bit older and was a little bit bigger then. And nice things too. I could, I thought, teach him how to throw ninja stars, and it would be, I thought, fun to have someone to play GI Joes with.

So Mom and I had this bet that if the baby was a girl I'd do all the house cleaning for a full year and if the baby was a boy, she'd buy me a Lamborghini Testarossa when I turned sixteen. I'd remind her every day about it. Sometimes, I'd hear her call my name. I'd be like, yelling back, "What?" and she'd be like, "Just come here, idiot!" And I'd go around and find her, wherever she was, and usually she was scrubbing the toilet, or spraying the trash can with the hose, or holding up Dad's stinky underwear. "Hope you remember that bet," she'd say, pinching her nose, and I'd run away, screaming.

I remember hearing her on the phone with Dad, having a kind of serious discussion. She looked fine to me, but she told him she was bleeding. I asked her what's wrong. I didn't see any blood, and I was an expert, even then. She just hung up, waved me toward her and said, "You're a good kid," into my ear. "You have a good heart." And I remember crying because she was crying, hanging onto me for dear life. And because I just knew the bet was off.

*

We've been driving for about an hour through Chicago's toll-choked upper limits when I try playing a Stones cassette I'd found on the floor, but Vince's tape deck munches it up. We're cruising along quietly for a little bit when he goes, "Why'd you leave, Ant?"

"Like it's some state secret."

"Mall gig money not enough for you?"

"Should it have been? Should I have been grateful for the privilege of playing Rudolph the Red-Nosed Reindeer in front of a Cinnabon for the rest of my life while some dead-eyed teen in an elf get-up clangs a bell for Salvation Army donations?"

"You know what we all think?"

"There's not enough roofers in Algonquin?"

"We think you're embarrassed by us. We think you're ashamed."

"Who's 'we' exactly? Why're you bringing this up now?"

"Just making conversation. We got a ways to go still and I thought—what better time to drill down to the heart of things?"

"How about later?"

"When suits you?"

"When's the moon finally escaping earth's gravity?"

"Have to check…"

"You check and get back to me."

"We treat you like one of ours, you know."

"Lucky me."

"Caroline thinks you're in trouble."

"I don't talk to Caroline so I don't know what she's getting at."

"She hears things. We all do. Even Uncle Josef."

"Hear whatever you want. Uncle Josef? He's digging a bunker in his backyard, did you all hear about that?"

"You know, we could've been cold."

"Yes, and I could've been a roofer in Algonquin. Gosh, maybe even a carpenter. Who knows, if I'm lucky, maybe get my balls zapped one day. Look, I left because I just left. It seemed like the thing to do. Sue me." I started to laugh.

"You know what you smell like?"

"Does this tape deck do anything other than mangle tapes? You got an aux cord or something in back? I can plug in the Discman."

"You smell like death, Ant. You've got it all over you."

"Why don't you just drive and keep your eyes on the road?"

"Dee-ee-ay-tee-aych. You stink of it."

"Good to know. Thank you for pointing that out. Anyway, you got your answer."

It's quiet again, but I can't quite leave it alone. I happen to like the way I smell.

"...Seriously though. Do I?"

"You and me both, brother. We reek of it." He starts laughing, the laughing becomes hacking, he hawks something up, and he swallows it back down.

*

Before I moved away, I visited my grandparents, Paul and Dorothy, one last time. When I was a kid they had owned a meek and merry home with cable TV, a pool table in the basement, and toward the back, a hovel my grandfather had fashioned from stacked electronic and radio equipment—requisitioned from his days in the Air Force and then as a company man at Motorola—wherein he would while the hours away, tinkering, lit by the blue-white flashes of his soldering iron.

They didn't have any toys, though. Visiting them as a boy, I'd quickly exhaust my imagination playing with whatever I'd brought with me from home. I would moan and groan to my grandmother that there was nothing to do. I was so bored.

Sometimes I bugged her to the point where she'd put me in her lap and we'd explore the back issues of *National Geographic* magazine they had dutifully collected over the years.

I learned about the long-necked women of the Maasai and their lion-stalking men. I saw Kenya's grand and wicked creatures—the jackal and croc, the wildebeest and laughing hyena. "I want to go there," I would say.

"That would be nice," she would reply, turning the page.

I learned about Tokyo, Hawaii, the Yukon, Mongolia, saw macaws as blue as lobsters, the petunia-petal skirts of Istanbul's dervishes, violet wildflower prairie fields, deserts at the bottom of the sea.

We agreed to visit them all. Over the years, we even made it to one or two—Cahokia Mounds, Mammoth Cave—though they weren't as moving as the pictures.

By the time I made that last visit, they'd swapped their home and everything in it for a condo, had both weathered numerous open-heart surgeries. Grandpa, the imperfect excision of a brain tumor. She had become fragile, he'd lost his marbles, and both needed a nurse in the home to keep them up and running.

I brought them McDonald's cheeseburgers, fries, and Cokes. We ate, the golf game on mute, played rummy until the sun was just a pink cuticle barely making it over some far-off trees.

I lost the last round. And when that happened, Grandpa laughed like a young man, a specific chuckle he had that I tried to mimic to perfection, and thus keep forever in my head. A humble, knowing, easy laugh of a man thankful for the blessed fortune life graced him with. Then he slipped back into his dementia as I collected the cards and wiped the string of saliva from his mouth. And though they were alive, I cried in the shower when I got home. Six months later, when they were both dead, it felt like yesterday's news.

Now, with the sunset's cider glow banished to the lip of the imperial sky's horizon, it's easy to feel the end of the world is near. The freeway's clotting with outbound traffic; the local streets below it are blue and empty now. The city looks to be on its last legs, has the feel of Pompeii.

As the shadows lengthen, earlier and longer each day, I'm imagining them remaining that way for all time. I sometimes think we have instincts guiding us away from our personal or collective extinction, or luring us toward it. Or simply one single instinct that tells us it's there, that the end is coming, wherever it may be at the moment. The atmospheric pressure is bombing out. It leaves the kind of cold that could split skin if you go gloveless very long and catch a wrap on the knuckles. The kind of cold that chaps nostrils. The air can barely hold onto the earth. Even the cars look miserable out there—unwashed, wretched masses queuing up for the succor of a bread heel, every last tailpipe chain-smoking as gridlock sets in.

I tell Vince to pull off somewhere because his check engine light's on, but it should have been obvious, given his car's state of disrepair—the light's been lit like that for ages.

"I check the engine all the time," he says, "and know what I see? A freaking engine."

"Check engine means there's something wrong. Like, low oil, or a belt's about to break or something."

"That's what the oil light's for. Think I don't know how to drive?"

"I'm not saying anything…"

"Ah, c'mon. I'm joking. These days cars are all electronics and they short sometimes. Nah, the engine's good to go. I had a guy look at it just last week."

"Okay, good to know, you could've said that."

"Had the guy change the oil, the filters, put air in the tires. I even filled up on wiper fluid."

"Fine, I got it. I'm just saying how come the light's on, that's all."

"The guy fixed the engine light, he—"

"Then why is it *on*?"

"Because he said it might come back on sometimes but to not worry about it because it's just the dang *electronics* in cars these days and that it doesn't matter the fucking engine's *fine*!"

Vince accelerates, takes the off-ramp at a borderline lethal velocity. I have to grip the handle not to knock heads with him. He just barely misses clipping a Lexus parked in the gas station lot we pull into.

"Know what? I don't deserve this kind of grief, man. You act like I'm this kind of drooling *window* licker. But guess what? I'm actually pretty smart. I know what I'm doing."

"All right, Christ…"

"You know, the other day I'm driving home from work and I have to run a few errands. Catherine needs some saline solution or some shit, and Caroline wants to do Mongolian barbecue for dinner because we got a new Mongolian barbecue place—what's wrong with regular barbecue? I don't know, but what else is there to do, so I went and had to go pick that up because she'd called in the order early so as to time it all perfect and keep it all hot by the time it gets home, so I go into the drug store and I buy the stupid contact solution—the buy one get one pack—and I book over to 75th Street to go get the food order for Caroline, and I'm driving home, I'm turning onto our street and there's Ray and Bullets."

"Let's talk and drive. Let's go, Vince, c'mon—"

"No, you listen—I see Ray, and I see Bullets. Ray's on the ground, no jacket, no shirt, no nothin'. It's winter. The snow around them's—sort of pink. I'm out of the car and going over, and the minute I lock eyes on Bullets he gets all low over Ray, and starts growling these don't-fuck-with-me growls. Ray's not moving. He is *out*, like he just got clocked by I don't know. And Bullets—someone'd painted clown makeup or something on his face, all over his muzzle. A clown dog. Or like he'd maybe gone and snatched one of Mom's cobblers and eaten it all up. Then it hits me what's happening."

"Let's go, man. You don't—"

"I stop walking. I do that, and Bullets quits growling at me. He starts panting, smiling."

"Vin, you were in shock. You maybe still are. Just calm down…"

"The frontal, temporal, and occipital scalp had multiple, predominately superficial, incised wounds, puncture wounds, and abrasions. The largest incised wound penetrated approximately 1.8 centimeters into the soft tissues and muscles of the right side of the neck."

"I get it…"

"What else. Oh, the soft tissues and muscles of the right side of the neck were hemorrhagic. Multiple axillary vessels were severed in the left forearm. Patches of neck and chest soft tissue exhibited muscle hemorrhage, multiple rib fractures, left hemothorax—whatever *that* is—"

"*Stop.*"

"—Contusions of the left lung, contusions of the heart. Is what the autopsy said. I read it enough I got parts memorized. But I couldn't tell any of that at the time though. I couldn't tell anything, except he looked really bad. The dog opened him up. Happy now?"

Vince cuts the engine and gets out.

"*You* calm down."

He slams the door and storms off, leaving me in the car, where I can feel the semis barrel past.

I'm filling the tank and to pass the time, I also fill the back-seat windows with pentagrams and wobbly smiley faces finger-scraped into the salty frost-grime encrusting the glass, as I wait for Vince to pay for gas inside.

When he waltzes back to the car, I give him a nod but he disregards it. So, as he's passing by the front of the car I spritz him with a little gasoline. Just a little bit, barely any—a couple flecks—get on his jeans.

"Don't you start *that* shit," he says, striding toward me. He can tell I'm playing, but still, he stops, then swipes a rainbow with his thumb across the windshield's schmutz. With that, he then smears an inverted cross along his brow. He gets right up in my face and does the same to mine.

"C'mon. Let's *party*," he says, wild-eyed, full of wry, old venom, and even though he's back, I can't tell if he's joking.

*

The engine dies about twenty miles later. We just paid a toll and we're on the pike, getting back on 94 when the lights go out, and suddenly it feels like we're sailing between the tall walls of an Arctic gully, the snow gray as old crazy glue.

What makes it bad is that that particular turnpike is one of those that has a stoplight, to help mitigate traffic snarls, that lets cars on little by little, like micro doses of antidote, time-released into the main artery.

We need to get out and push and there's a line about ten cars deep behind us, each about ten seconds from losing it.

The blast of air shuts down my lungs the instant I open the door.

"Hit the hazards, Vince."

"What hazards?"

"You know what I just thought of? Someone's got to steer."

We are veering, foot by foot, toward that filthy, salty snow bank cresting along the shoulder. The front headlight makes contact just as Vince slides behind the wheel, too late to not get halted dead in our tracks. I yell for him to cut it left, hard, and when that does nothing, to get out and be useful for once.

"I gotta steer, I thought!" he yells back.

"Do *both*. We're running—*aground*."

The cars in back of us barely pause. We soon clear the snow bank, but it's almost a quarter mile to the next exit. It'd take all night for a tow truck to get here, were there a phone nearby to even call one.

The effort feels like one of those running-in-slow-motion dreams. I locate a cauldron of anger inside me, I kick it over and push that heap on and on and on. The frigid metal numbs the heels of my palms. Whenever the highway traffic quiets or the wind lets up, it sounds like we're lethargically steamrolling over a blanket of bugs.

With my eyes to the asphalt, I grind it out. I had told myself on the plane, this funeral, this service—it had better be worth it. I'd wanted the full payload dropped on my head, to emerge core-shook and sparkling, death-ecstatic, fully diamond-hearted. But this feels all wrong, beyond my sphere of control. Everything's upside down; there are cruel stars of road salt underfoot. I ought to be gung ho, chomping at the bit. Instead, I'm shoving a dead sedan along a shoulder, crossing lines I should not be, wondering: what's waiting at the end of this road, is it too late to turn back, who's the real dimwit here?

When I pop my head up again, Vince is back in the car, waving to the passersby in his dusty admiral coat like some kind of weird pageant winner.

He checks the rearview mirror and when he catches me doing my best to telepathically burst him into flames he ducks low in his seat. "Vince I can still *see* you, fucking muppet…"

As the car slows and lists, I sneak to the door. "How about it's time we switch."

"I only got one *hand*, hot shot."

"Use your elbow or something." I start yanking him by the collar and he relents. The cold is so cold it's like an awl in your ear. As a shield the car door is a joke against the bitter windscream. With everything I've got, I plant one foot, then the next, and push to make it end.

"Wel—come home!" Vince cries.

*

Batteries don't die on running engines but here we are.

"Battery." That is all we get from the mechanic as he lets down the hood with a clap. Vince and I shiver against the garage wall, burning our tongues on bland cocoa from the vending machine, puddles forming at our feet as we defrost.

"How much is a replacement?" Vince says.

The guy gets stern as a doctor, scribbling notes on a thick metal clipboard. "Duralasts run about one-fifty," he says. "Valucraft's less. Around one-twenty-five, one-thirty."

Vince gives me a look.

"With labor," the guy goes on, "that's maybe another hundred. Might not have any Valucraft left. Have to see in back."

"Why don't you go check in the back and see if you got any, and then we'll see about which battery we want."

"Should have 'em..." The guy says, and walks off.

Vince leans back and sighs. "Battery."

"Just get the damn Durlalast and let's get the hell out of here."

"I should call Caroline."

"She's just going to say what I just said."

"How do you know?"

"You know how I know? I know because the both of us hate mechanics, garages, cars, and most of all, how much it sucks waiting around for them to get fixed."

He sees the wisdom of this, if him shutting up is any indication. But when the guy comes back and tells us it's our lucky day, Vince looks around, says, "You guys don't have a phone I could use to make a quick call, do you?"

"I'll cover the spread," I tell him.

"What's that?"

"Don't make me repeat myself."

"Seems it *is* my lucky day after all," he says, beaming at the guy.

"Fine by me. Go grab a seat in the lounge over there, if you two want to wait."

"How long'll it be?" I ask.

"Not long."

"Oh," I say, "that's not bad..."

"I love lounges," Vince says. "Look, this one even has a *Playboy* calendar. Classic."

"Nothing happens in them. Not even sleep," I say. Downing the dregs of my insipid cocoa, I settle into my chair and listen to an air wrench zing the lugs off a Toyota's tire someone felt the need to slash.

*

About ten minutes stewing in the lounge, with Vince humming along to Empire carpet TV commercials, I'm pretty ready to swallow my tongue. I head outside, kick an ice chunk around the parking lot until it's a hockey puck, then nothing more than a poker chip.

He looked just like he did outside the principal's office. I wonder if the little portable TV the secretary had propped on the file cabinet by her desk was the secret reason he got in trouble so often. It wasn't so rare to catch sight of him there, taking in a little *Price is Right*, as I headed to the bathroom, or between class.

"What they get you for?" I'd ask.

"*Pfft*. Petty theft."

Once we're good to go, the guy yells us over, I write out a check, and they bring the car around.

"Mind if I drive?" I ask. Vince gets all still.

"I don't know," he says. "This is a 1987 Cutlass Supreme. Not for amateurs."

"Who knows that better than me? C'mon. Just to get food."

"You even know how to drive still?"

I start the engine and Vin buckles up, digs a joint out of his shirt pocket. Clenching it between his teeth, he pats himself down for a light. He's got the business end twisted like a Tootsie Roll, and when Vince sparks it, the flame stays there, the joint a little birthday candle until he blows it out and takes a giant toke.

"Are we hot-boxing this thing?" I say, putting us in reverse, then letting in some fresh air. "Gonna drive us right smack into the first fucking wall I see. Cannot wait."

"Hold on a sec," Vince says. "Don't go yet." He grows silent, cocks an ear. "Just listen to that baby purr…"

"Let me know when you're ready…"

Vin puts his seat back a few notches until he's just a pair of dark pink eyes peeking out. He hits the defroster, breathes out another cloud.

"Okay," he says. "Ready."

The oasis off the main exit is cut into four quadrants by the north-south Tri-State and some junction running perpendicular to it, which branches off into other routes and avenues that trickle into the little suburbs and hamlets carved from shallow pockets of farmland and forest.

At the turn out, waiting on traffic, Vince points off at a pair of gas stations and burger chains on the other side of the exit. "I'd recognize that big red cowboy hat a dozen miles away," he says.

"I can smell the curly fries."

Vince hands me the joint. "You need to hit this."

"Maybe later on."

"You sure? It's dipped in a little of this embalming fluid stuff a buddy scored. Sounds harsh, but it's…" He just grins, searching for the word. "…a love boat. Says it all."

"Tempting, but I think I'll maybe pass…"

Each quadrant is no more than a few hundred yards long, and even less than that lies between them. Nevertheless, we've been in the Cutlass for more than fifteen minutes, I've driven maybe fifty feet. The cross-traffic may as well be an Amtrak train.

Vince gnaws at a hangnail, spits it like a sunflower shell.

"You got something on your mind," I say.

"Swear I just saw a bird."

I peer into the dark. "You have some keen vision…"

"Thought it was one I'd seen before. When your grandpa was in the hospital. It'd been raining non-stop all night. So it was a pretty morning—breezy, kind of loose, with big, almost-blue clouds moving fast. Just as I look out the window, a great big white seagull flies by. And I thought, *man…*"

I can feel the earnest look he casts at me, but I keep my eyes on the left turn signals blinking across the road.

"Your grandpa's last words," he says. "Know what they are?"

I don't want to know, but I look at him anyway. He is staring into the lights now, knuckling out a little beat on the window.

"Said: Play the trumpets, and cheer us up."

"Doesn't sound like him."

"I think he thought I was you."

I almost miss my chance to go when it's our turn. The bald wheels spin, burning rubber. We begin fishtailing into that no man's land in the middle of the intersection.

I have to lay off the pedal completely, then press again, with the weight of a few feathers, until the tires stick. I hold out my hand to Vince. The joint's just a roach by this point. But it hits like a champ. And I'm hearing trumpets now. I'm seeing birds everywhere.

*

Vince follows me into the restaurant, where everything is humming, backlit, lacquered yellow and brown molded plastic, and screwed to the floor.

I'm feeling pretty cosmic until making eye contact with the girl behind the counter, whose look is a katana that vivisects us as we're blundering in like a couple flushed crackheads thinking they own the place. Her stare is cool and withering. I feel caught naked.

"Welcome to Arby's," she says to me.

"Huh? I mean—thank you. It's good to be here..."

"Qasra—what kind of name's that?" Vince says.

"Kashmiri. It means—do you want to order something to eat or not."

"Lemme get a number five," I say.

"What size would you like."

"Oh, man. Um, let's go with medium. Vince, know what you want?"

"I can't decide between all this shit..."

"When you know what you want, just let me know," she says.

"Two 38s," I tell her.

"Hold it!"

Qasra smacks her gum. Vince, wincing at the menu like a paranoid dyslexic. In the corner, someone is shrouded in a sleeping bag, bare feet propped up near the napkins and condiments. Beyond him and us, the place is empty.

"Not usually this indecisive. Must be the herb," Vince says, but suddenly, Qasra's all ears.

"Trade you food for some," she says. Yet even now, her detached expression doesn't change.

Vince nudges me, leans in close. "This a sting operation, what you think? Be surprised how often that goes down..."

I nudge him back, away from me.

"Hurry up," she says. "Are we cool?"

"Well, what's a joint good for?"

"One room-temperature roast beef, plus a large fries."

"...Curly or regular."

"I can do curly."

"Fries fresh?"

"Fresh for this place. What about your smoke."

I say, "You sure this is the time and place for this?"

"Who asked you, ugly?"

Vince laughs. "Will you marry me? I mean, I'm already married, but at least come with us up to Big Bend? I could use you in the car, help keep the peace."

Qasra considers this. "That sounds like the start of an awful slasher flick."

Before returning to the menu, he mumbles, "Awfullest slasher flicks were always the best."

Boredom sets her eyes wandering. She's about four feet tall. I think she'd yawn if a sabretooth rolled in on a skateboard. Vin finds his eighth, taps the rolled Ziploc on the counter.

"I'll roll you three for two burgs, two curlies, and two large Dr. Peppers."

Qasra punches in our order. "Coming right up," she says. "Dad! I'm going for my break now..." From behind the fryer, an older man looks out to the front, but there's only Qasra's apron there.

We head back out to the car. I get in shotgun. He and Qasra slide in back. She keeps her door open.

"How's work?" I ask.

"Incredibly amazing in every way."

"Cool..."

"I don't have all night."

"Let's go, Vince."

"Are you guys poor or something?"

Neither of us respond. In the rearview, I watch Vince break up lime green nuggets on an upturned Frisbee with the focus of a bench jeweler.

"You guys on the run? Someone after you? The law? The mob?"

"Be quiet," Vin says, concentrating on his craft. Qasra gears up to unload on him, but holds off.

"There a motel or anything nearby?" I ask.

"Um," she says, "if you can read, just check out the signs off the highway. They say what's around."

"I know how to *read*, I just—Vince? Any day now. I've got to take a leak."

"The restroom is out of service. A customer went nuts in there earlier."

"One down, two to go. Voila," He says, placing the joint in her palm. She barely glances at it before getting it good and roasting.

"There's a port-a-potty over there," she says, and points to a pair of them teeming with icicles long as tusks beside the dumpster in the parking lot next door. "It is—functional. You got like a—emergency?"

"Almost done here. I'll get our food," Vince says.

I give him a thumbs up and split.

It's dark and stinks of urinal cakes. The ventilator fan blades chop up a street lamp's orange glow, and it's like whizzing in a silent film. The hand soap looks like phlegm. No paper towels, no toilet paper, obviously.

When I get out, Qasra's by the curb, snacking on a bag of Sour Patch Kids, whimsically faded. She is lightly swaying on her heels to music that isn't there, cocooned in some warm personal thoughts that seem to stave off the cold.

"Wait now, just a minute—seriously, what are you two about?" she asks me. Her hand goes to my chest, stopping me as I'm about to push open the restaurant door.

"About? What's that mean?"

"You and the other one. I can see it on your faces, how you walk... like you've been sentenced. Like you're on your way to the gulag. Call me crazy."

"Okay, you're crazy." I give a nice-guy smile, and Qasra knows it's a nice-guy smile. Nice, clean, empty, fake.

But I don't want to say, don't want to get into it and spoil the nice feeling I'd been enjoying, and it dawns on me it was because Ray had slipped from my mind. Just like that. Just like years ago, until I turned on the TV last week and remembered, was forced to remember, how far apart the houses were, that a baseball diamond stood just down the block, with a chain link fence that drooped, trash drums always crawling with wasps, across the street from Bad's, all the do-nothing hangs we had outside its doors, watching skateboarders practice popping ollies off the curb until their elbows and knees were bloody patches—me, Vince, Ray, scrawny-looking in our XL K-mart t-shirts—all I could do nothing about.

I tell her we're on a pilgrimage. I tell her it's nothing sad, no big deal, bit of cabin fever, more like an errand, a business trip practically, pretty boring, nothing worth mentioning, might catch a show but we don't know yet, nothing's final, just going to play it by ear. I know I've failed miserably at something the moment I finish all my telling. Qasra's little hand drops, she gestures *oh well*, pirouettes away from me, and I hurry back inside.

"She said a dude had a seizure or like an episode or something in there earlier," Vince tells me when I sit down.

"Just one?"

He takes a chomp of his roast beef.

As we're eating, a family in the back, who must've come in while we were in the car, is getting ready to leave when their toddler chucks a baby fistful of horsey sauce packets at the sleeping guy, and the mom scrambles to fetch them. Her guy keeps his eyes hidden by the bill of his Fighting Irish cap. When the toddler slaps the table, he gives it crayons.

"What happened to Gavin anyway?" I ask.

"You miss him?"

"Please, chew your food. Was just wondering. He still living with his grandma?"

"Granny Kwasneski's gotta be dead as a doornail by now, I would think. I don't talk to them—haven't spoken to her or him in years. I do know he got swept up by police the night his mutt attacked Ray. Who knows what they're going to do with him. Won't be enough, whatever they got in store."

"Probably hit him with reckless endangerment, negligence, something along those lines."

"What they should do is hit him with a cinderblock."

"Thought you were a pacifist."

"Tell me to ease up, Ant. Tell me to chill. See what you get hit with."

"Boy, you sure are bloodthirsty…"

Vince takes another big bite. When he swallows, he seems to swallow his wrath down, too, dismissing his threat with an eye roll, a shake of the head. Like he always used to do.

The guy in the corner makes a shriek like someone just stomped him. He glares around the restaurant in wide-eyed outrage.

"Who in the hell are you?" He bellows at us, "What are you doing?"

Qasra strides back in from out front. "Bijan, shut it. You had a bad dream, that's all."

"It was no dream. I know what you're trying to do."

"Let's get out of here," Vince says.

He clears his tray into the garbage quickly to avoid notice, and I'm behind him, wishing he'd go quicker.

"Hey, you," Bijan says, wriggling free of his sleeping bag. He gets up in my face, clutches my arm, not like he's going to hit me or anything, but like he's got something urgent to say. I kind of just let him do it.

"You're not fooling me. You're not fooling *any*body," he says.

"I'm not trying to…" I say, and give a yearbook portrait smile. Vince is honking in a kind of Morse code for "Let's Go."

"He doesn't mean anything by that, he's—you know…" Crossing her eyes, Qasra winds her finger around her ear.

Bijan approaches the window. Cupping his hands around his face, he looks out to Vince, who is basically leaning on the horn now. But he can wait. I'm beginning to come down.

"I'm glad you work at Arby's. It's my favorite fast food restaurant. That's not a lie."

As I'm walking out I hear, "I have made that pilgrimage before, you know…"

I stop.

"…It's bullshit."

At that moment she is wildly believable to me, and then her father takes over the register.

*

From the hotel just off the Edens pike you can hear the change being tossed at the toll plaza glowing orange in the surrounding darkness. We lurk through the parking lot, seeking an empty spot.

"The marquee says vacancies," Vince says, but I'm holding my breath, fearing a jinx and more driving.

"So. Qasra, huh."

"That's her name," Vince says.

"Must be tough, working at the slowest Arby's in the world."

"Poor thing."

"Food was good at least."

"It's Arby's. You can't not eat good at Arby's."

"There!" I shout, pointing out an empty parking space which might be handicapped but who cares.

We get out and Vince's like, "Go get us a room, I'm gonna polish off this pinner real quick."

After snagging the last bed they have, I check out the view from the little balcony. There is not much to see. Vin's down there babbling to himself between the parked cars and the rail guard separating the lot from the frozen island toll barrier. Rehearsing a joke, or an excuse.

He has no idea what room we're in, nor that I am observing him. If I were still high, the traffic might be more entertaining. I might launch a snow ball, a soda bottle, an ice bucket, if I were still high and had any one of those items.

He's slowly wobbling around in circles, head back, gawking at some light blinking in the sky. I can just make out his lips moving as he then gazes down at that roach between his fingers.

"Hey, stupid!"

That gives him a start, and he looks around like he just received the word of God.

I give a wave.

Vince dabs the roach to his tongue, stumbling toward the red wrought iron stairs leading up to room 229.

*

They're out of cots. Vince claims the bed so I sprawl on the floor. Before we hit the hay, he can't relax until he rings Caroline up.

"—Sure. Sure. Ant?" he says.

Vince clubs me in the head with a throw pillow.

"—Ant's the same, we're getting along fantastic, things are fine. Wouldn't you say, Ant?" He's nodding his head yes.

"—What else? Oh—put a new battery in the whip.

"—Because. Just—because, all right? It's just responsible car ownership. It was time for a replacement. Because I keep track of things like this.

"—Put June Bug on.

"—Hey there. Being a good girl for Mom? Say that again, I didn't hear…

"—Who told you that? Who put that in your head?

"—Hello?"

"She hang up on you?" I ask.

He looks at me, amazed. "'Dada, do you love me still?' Can you believe a question like that?"

"You sound shook."

"Well you wonder where a five-year-old kid gets these ideas," he says. He waits for some kind of answer, but I'm still thinking about June's question, how the call just ended out of the blue.

"Just call them back then, like a normal human being."

He dials again, brings the phone with him as he paces, waiting for the line to connect. "Still ringing," he says.

"I see that."

"I don't know, man, I don't like this…"

"Quit overreacting."

"—Hey, Caroline. Sorry, I think we got disconnected. Everything good over there?"

"—Because I don't know, June said something…"

"—She—never mind. It doesn't matter. I'll see you soon."

"—Okay, night."

"You're a good father," I tell him. He rolls his eyes, timbers into bed like a felled redwood. I click off the lamp.

"Tomorrow'll be pretty hard," he says into the quiet. I'm listening to the tinnitus whine in my ears—it's a weird comfort—hoping my silence is taken to mean I'm out. "It's going to be terrible, don't you think?"

"I think it'll be okay." I yawn.

"Probably right. What's the big deal? Just burying a kid. Big whoop. Sure it'll be a real heart-warmer. Did live a long and productive life, after all. Spent his days on this earth doing good works. Could've been worse. Went peacefully in his sleep, at least. Not a bad way to bite the dust. Oh. Hold up. That's 89-year-old cousin Phil. My mistake. We're talking about the torn-apart-by-a-pit-bull kid. Nah, yeah, it'll be pretty mellow."

"I kind of like funerals," I say.

"Yeah, you would, creep."

"They might be my favorite thing."

"You're a sick fuck, Ant. Pleasant dreams. Try not to have too much fun tomorrow. His mother'll be there."

A little while later I hear, "Ant. *Ant.*"

I'm through faking sleep now. "Just talk, Vince. Why you need to have me say 'what'? Just go."

"I was just wondering. I keep forgetting. What is it that you're doing out there now anyway? You still play?"

"Thought you'd never ask."

"...Well?"

"You did. I was wrong."

"Oh, lord... sorry for asking. Wasn't bad, having music in the house all the time. Your practicing got aggravating as hell but now I miss it. Kind of. Don't make fun of me."

"...I play when I can. That isn't very often. In the downtime, I work where I can. Temping. Substitute teach, now and then. I don't mean to be a prick. Wish I had some kind of spectacular answer for you."

"Ah, you're keeping secrets..."

We're silent for a while, but I can sense he's brooding. It's too quiet.

"Tell me," I say.

"I just remember thinking," he says, "looking at that dog—he was lording over Ray, like, you know, a lion over a kill. I thought, Jesus Christ, that's—I am looking at Death itself, live, in the flesh. That was what went through my mind. Felt like I was face to face with... not a dog. Not *just* a dog."

I sit up, strain my eyes to fix on Vince through the fuzzy gloom. "That's not so weird to me, Vince."

We go back to being fake-asleep.

In the dark before sleep comes I watch the floral wallpaper abstract to become different patterns, the ceiling's mild rippling stucco, hear the heat come on like a fire touching off. I like how headlights coming through the windows sweep the room like a copy machine, and when it's dark before sleep to think about Wendy.

We'd drink from the same cup, she and I in the morning before leaving for our dumb jobs—a mug of green tea that would get lukewarm, hardly had, or she would make coffee with the special press of hers I never figured out how to use. Our mug read "Might Be Gin." She found it in a picnic basket of crap outside an empty home's aluminum mailbox, left by someone who moved away for good and didn't have room. We were just hitting our kitschy knick-knack prime.

I would drink my share, long sips now and then, before forgetting about it, then she would pick it up, drink her portion, and forget about it, and that's how mornings went between Wendy and me.

And I would see her off with our secret little handshake.

I like digging them up, all of these pointless specifics. I like to think about Wendy the way I like to pick at scabs, peeling off the dead parts until I draw a bead of blood, a bright scarlet pinhead. I like doing this, at night, in the quiet, picking away the necrotic rind of my heart stinging fresh, and I feel something real again at least.

That Labor Day she snapped my photograph in the backyard for no real reason. A precise flower blend I could never pinpoint, which her side of the bed smelled of to me. The night she poked fun at me in front of everyone and we were wine drunk and she placed her temple to mine and gave me amnesia. How it was as simple for her to just quit, shelve it all and go as getting the mail, because it was better that way. I curl into the hurt like a stiff, dead leaf, and listen.

A specific sound will catch and pull me inside out, like a shirt-sleeve hooking on a twist of fence. The rummage for correct change in a leather purse, perhaps. A sniffle, an uproar, muttered swear words at the front-door lock that you have to have the magic touch to make work.

The lowlight reel returns. Further back, more backward, until she will stroll my way, a benevolent sorceress in old blue pumas, and it's the day Wendy walks right past my table, trailing the perfume of the orange she'd just eaten. Then everything works out right, I think, lying to myself. A low form of necromancy, I'd claim, *that is*, she'd reply with a wink, *just routine masochism in the end.*

Sometimes the hurt will gush, as if she and I collapsed only an hour ago, or stun me stupid like the last time, when I was one of dozens, maybe hundreds, who were missing her, dumbstruck where they stood, having expected to go on seeing her for a long time and we were all wrong.

I think about all that I have expected that turned out to be wrong, in the dark before sleep, remind myself the joy and love and success found by all the regular people I know are not meant for me, and when I remind myself of this, I can picture the look on my face, and would prefer no one sees it.

I recall, at night, when we had finally severed our lives from one another, how she hoped I was happy, wanted the best for me and how that stunk like a lie. How her generosity was the worst part, and how thinking *that* is the worst part is not good. Not good. I remember thinking I hope she's miserable. That I hope she's devastated I'm devastated. That she is listless and guilt-ridden, judged by her friends, who, I remember thinking, surely were on my side, knew I was the good guy in all this. The *victim*. That she cannot, for the life of her, figure out what she did to draw their disdain. For the life of her. What my bitterness cost I'll never manage to calculate. The debt appreciates. I'd rather not know.

I'm listening, keeping watch for the burnt orange sky to freckle with stars, for them to offer some kind of solace, even though I absolutely know better than to expect anything other than deeper cold, more raps on the snout for hoping a change in luck is just around the corner. *What are you looking at us for?* the stars seem to say. *We thought you were someone else.*

Until I start thinking I should grow up, for all sorts of reasons, but in tonight's case, because of Ray. Because it is vile, because it is disgraceful. But the inertia of my self-pity propels me on, this is the perfect setting for thoughts such as these—here where they will not spread or spoil the days and moods of less troubled people. Here I let them roam, where it is dark and warm enough to incubate these monstrous hopes and regrets and wishes and tastes, and enable their growing up big and strong and cruel, into the Gavin Kwasneskis this great state must one day reckon with.

Wendy would probably disagree, if she were here, too. Where I see a beyond-drunk maniac speeding to make the light, hit Wendy and run, Wendy would have just seen some lady named Regina driving home from happy hour, who had to pee really bad and just a few blocks to go. She would remind me conjuring maniacs is my quaint attempt at sparing myself the grief mundane truth is always screwed into.

In the dark I should know there is very little stopping one from cold-blooded appraisals of all the catastrophes and thefts and faults your life sops up, and how, and why, and you, your part in the job. Best to take a good look at yourself in dim light, when you are small, closest to sleep, to death, when I can almost feel it, I think, or feel anything, acknowledge that this is what is happening to me, that I can feel it happening, feel myself warping, my branches twisting, hardening my heart. And it is scary and dispiriting, yet it is a good feeling too. How good it feels to have nothing to fear, nothing tender left, not a single weak spot, to understand you are soon to be what the miserable world dreads and teaches its children to beware. It is thrilling, I think, enough to keep me awake in the dark all night long.

I was sure is the point. About her, I was always certain. That was the problem. And the point was we had, were supposed to have, plenty of time. Wendy, who wasn't even my wife—yet—she was never always anything. The point was I knew. The problem was Wendy, seeing that, let the world continue its swerve toward her. If there is some kind of cosmic lesson in this I refuse to learn it.

Vince is retching in the bathroom, hacking up a lung. Half-awake, I crack open one eye, in the heavy static dark and look: outside, in the sky, very far away, see the bright grain of light I came so close to? Just a plane, lit like a comet, distant enough to appear stock-still.

I think I'll ask whether Vince worries in similar fashion, at night, in his bed, beside Caroline, if she wards off his disquiet, if he prays that nothing steals the largesse of human care and tenderness in which crude Vince is cushioned, like a bubble-wrapped tomahawk. Does it trouble him and if it does, does he pray and worry if and when his present circumstances might change? Is he afraid of earthquakes?

Possibly we are both shook, and still shaking. And I consider whether I have simply come to feed off the shame of being a walking tragedy. And I wonder what Dan and Marcy wonder in their bed, how they keep from quaking the whole night through, if they even bother trying now.

And before I crash out I'm recalling all of them—Grandpa, blown mind. Grandma, bum ticker. Kid brother/sister-to-be, lost on the vine. Mom, Dad, dead, and dead to me, Wendy—and how each and every time, it left me a little more nerve-dumb, wracked with shivers, more familiar with the cold-blooded wash that seizes up the body, leaves me blue as a newborn just before the smack. I could see it coming, my being the last one left—over here was me, and over there? Everyone else, a million battalions of strangers—and what that all implies, and how crazy simple it is, finally, to convince myself I am just a weird remainder. How zero times anything always equals zero, and why more than anything else that makes me feel somehow special, which would probably make Wendy chime, *Sure, just like everybody else*, I think, and I'm just about to counter that part of me playing Wendy that I'm arguing with, the part of me I know I'll lose happily lose to once again, when Vince emerges out of the gloom like some deep-sea monster and shakes my shoulder in the groggy panic of a tranquilized kidnap victim just now coming to, asking me, "Hey, Ant, hey—they're okay, right? Everything's fine, right?"

"Who? What do you mean?"

But I know.

II

It was a Wednesday and I'd gone to the Food Bazaar, even though it was farther than Food Town, because it had a weekly special on gourmet frozen pizza. My groceries had shifted in the bag—the pineapple juice was squishing the donuts, but I was just about home. I got the door open right in time to catch the phone ringing.

Michael, her older brother. He was a Lutheran pastor. I listened and adjusted my food, chinning the receiver. Michael notified me about Wendy. First thing I said, "But she's going to be okay, right?"

He goes, "Beg your pardon?" But I lost the phone then, and my groceries next, and it took until the next morning, when my roommate Bob found the mess, to recall my stomping them both into the kitchen tile.

The day after I learned that Wendy Malone passed away, a fog crept into the city. It felt true. I, like the city, found myself in the throes of an endless opacity that made me and everyone else rub their eyes as they left their homes, so akin was the effect of that haze to cataracts, or night blindness. This all, I reasoned, was a natural phenomenon.

I sat down in my thinking chair, absorbing the news. I calculated the length of time since I'd last seen her. It came to around one year four months and that's as far as I got before I grew frantic and took off. I started to wander. The streets, overnight, had become ghostly basins inundated by that fog. I leapt as high as I could. Surely, someone, gazing out from some taller building's higher floor glimpsed my hand, I hoped.

Driving in this was lunatic, people muttered aloud to no one in particular at the bus stop by my house. Someone even yelled it at me from her ten-speed, seeing me plunge my car key into its lock. I smiled as I passed them, joyless.

I'd driven in worse, weather magnitudes worse than a dumb fog, I told myself. Through cold snaps, torrential downpours, beneath roiling green skies and lightning storms that assembled and struck at random.

I needed movement. Being stuck in the same spot turned my stomach. There was someplace I needed to be, inclement weather or not.

I was mostly lying to myself, naturally. I've never had an errand so urgent it called for chancing life and limb. But that was what it was—a vague tugging in my gut toward serious risk.

I got in my car and drove. Of course the funeral was a couple states away. Though it was mildly daunting to just leave everything and go, escaping the fog would be a comfort, I told myself, though that proved immaterial—night had fallen long before that cloudy broth dissipated.

By my sixth hour of straight driving, through two rush hours and one traffic snarl, my joints were too creaky and I was too famished to sustain even my aimless death wish, strong as it was, and found a motel with free HBO somewhere just inside the Pennsylvania state line.

All that time in the car left me feeling filmy and stale. I parked, paid, daydreamt about endless hot water. It felt like I was still driving when I finally got out, the landscape parallaxing as my feet hummed me past the motel's revolving glass doorway.

"That was some fog, wasn't it?" I said to the old woman at the desk, as I waited on the elevator.

"I think it's still there," she replied, engrossed in her word search. "You just can't see it."

I had a good, hour-long shower. The pressure was feeble, but it refreshed me to scrub off a bit of the distance I'd traveled. I felt a little regular again.

I remembered I had Dwight, my old friend. We used to work together at a brokerage—Bachman & Furth. Fellow office drones, him and I, doing what we could for rent money. He even met Wendy once or twice.

Dwight was right when he intoned, over the phone, "The roads are cake, it's the miles that rough you up." I asked if he knew of a bar somewhere near where I was. Once his daughter was born, he and Cindy, his wife, made for the hills outside the Poconos, thinking it a cleaner, safer, more sensible place where they could raise her up right.

"There are a few places, sure," he said.

"Grab a drink with me and let's catch up."

"Tomorrow's an early day for me. I would though."

"You've gone soft, old man. C'mon, how often am I out here?"

"Really, I can't. Cindy's got jury duty."

"Where's the *blood*lust, Dwight? The old apex predator of yore?"

"I've got to get Daisy to school. And you have no idea how picky she eats. I've got to make her lunch—"

"What'd they do to you? What happened to Dwight? Put *Dwight* on, Dwight the night rider, the high stakes gamblin' man."

"Ant—"

"I'm just giving you a hard time."

"Well, that makes sense."

"You know me, always agitating..." Catching the desperation in my own voice, I doubted I would want to drink with me either.

"Yeah, don't take this the wrong way. You're my boy, you know that. Maybe you ought to stay in though. Maybe try going soft on yourself, a little bit. It feels *nice*, believe it or not."

"Go hide out in the sticks the rest of my life, you mean? Blow off old friends when they come knocking?"

"Ant, listen to me—it truly sucks, what happened to Wendy. Take care of yourself. Clear skies are coming your way, I can feel it. You hear me? Hit me up on your way back through here. We'll get drunk as mops and go tie a hoe to a post."

I stayed up watching some talking heads dissect Iraq, mulling over what all Dwight said on the phone.

I had nothing left to lose. That's what it all boiled down to, and that began contorting the entirety of my grief, the more I continued focusing on it, what it really meant. I felt nausea like a cold tongue lick me. Getting up for a glass of water, my knees wobbled, but held out. I was standing, that felt like proof of something important. The last one standing.

It was as if, from out of nowhere, a supercell had gathered in the skies overhead and just as fast, just as inexplicably, dissipated. Wendy was gone. Just gone.

Who was left? I had sort of instinctively crouched, as though bracing myself for a beat down. But the storm never broke. Not a drop fell. It all felt childish. She was the last one. And everything I had hoped for, feared, wrestled with, regretted, daydreamt—it all fit snug in a kind of suitcase I'd kept in a closet in my heart that I was now free to hurl off a bridge. No one would see. There was nothing left to worry about. I was made whole.

The next morning I went home. If the fog was still there, I didn't even notice. The sickening hurt, the ten-ton depression, the vulnerability that left me hugging myself like a leper trying to stay in one piece as I drifted around town—it was all gone. I could breathe. I could see. I was almost too relieved to trust how I felt, expecting a relapse every ten minutes. But it endured. I was cured of it all. Everything but the death wish. The death wish blossomed. Laureled me in its pig-iron flowers. They were perfect—just the thing for funerals.

*

The sun is on the rise. I haven't really slept. Doubt Vince has either. On the little balcony, out over the rooftops, I watch chimney smoke flutter—ragged little white flags knotted to the pipes and stacks rising into the sky. Gray predawn winds drive a slab of clouds off.

I used to hate funerals—they were so *sad*.

So suffocating, really. A klieg light under which I had nothing to perform. No material. I would wander that agonizing stage, sweating buckets, dodging gazes seeking mine. So many hugs I still hate them, even now.

Mom, hollow-cheeked, a fixed-up mannequin, wig and all. The crowd surveilling me, waiting for me to do—what? I wanted to scream at them: Don't you get it? I was the one who *clapped*. The starlet is there, in that pine box. Is no more. Show's over.

I have all sorts of responses to the questions I ask myself as to why I go. They all nick the bull's eye. Specific, isolated reasons all cluster and gang up on me into this kind of preternatural, instinctual pull. Off I go, like a picnic basket carried away by a black river of ants, not caring why. Ambling through the wake, a kind of graduate, an old retired pro. Idling in the parlor, mute, holographic, negative space, loitering in the nave, burning the clock.

But there is something honest involved in each of my answers, to a varying degree, about The End, in the end.

Grandpa in the casket, hands folded at the waist, wearing what looked like Grandma's lipstick. Grandma smelling like talcum powder.

When I think about the truth involved in *that* answer, the answer to the big question of what's left after rendering down all these answers, I feel too close to a cliff within myself.

Everyone I thought invincible: shattered. Shell-shocked, asking each other what to do. All of them absolutely, in all honesty, clueless. We were all at a loss.

*

"I've attended three wakes in the past nine months or so," I say.

"Shocked you had three friends," Vince says, wrapping a black plastic bag around his bandaged hand before heading into the bathroom to shower.

He closes the door on me, but I keep talking. "Mr. Bachman, my old boss, in October, at the Cathedral of St. John the Divine. He was one of those slick Manhattan real estate giants. Place was crawling with agents and sharks. Everyone handing out business cards with their condolences. My bud Dwight made me go, to be honest."

"Shut *up*. Let me shower in peace."

"—But it was autumn, the city was gorgeous. The tree leaves were butterscotch, practically. Bachman was 93 for god's sake. I had no skin in the game. I left feeling like I'd just finished a perfect gourmet lunch. All nourished and fulfilled. I was happy, that afternoon. Glad I moved."

I continue. "Suzette Morelle was buried around Valentine's Day."

"Cousin Josef's wife. Heard about her," Vince calls from the shower.

"*Third* wife. I don't even remember ever meeting her before then. The Bachman service spoiled me. I got off the train that morning so stoked I had to talk myself down a little bit. Didn't want to spoil it. It was a great time though. They had a polka band, the catering was top flight, and drinks were on the house."

I hear him shut off the water.

"Too great, actually. A food fight broke out. Someone even hired a stripper. Suzette's brother-in-law suffered a coronary at the tail end of the night. Ambulance came. He ended up being okay, but it was almost a twofer."

When he finally gets out of the bathroom, Vince is clean shaven, wearing a two-piece charcoal suit a little too tight on him, and a pair of oxblood cowboy boots. It all somehow works.

"Those don't stick out at all."

Vince clears his throat. "Ray and me were into watching old Westerns when he was little. He was Clint, I was the bad dude. I dunno."

He stops me from heading in to shower myself.

"Let me tell you something: Suzette was a real person. She was actually really great," he says. "She was kind to me, even though she had no reason to. I didn't know her much at all. You got a big mouth, Ant. Keep it zipped if you got nothing good to say. It's hard being third anything. You bring any good clothes, or are you going to the chapel looking like a street person?"

"My dress clothes are in the trunk still. I forgot to bring up my bag."

"We're already running behind. Change on the way."

"What got into you?"

Vince starts to pack up his things.

"Let me brush my teeth first at least."

"You got two minutes." He sits on the bed, knots his laces.

"You got a brush I can use?"

"Packing is not a strength of yours, is it."

"Mine's also in my bag…"

"Wash it when you're done," he says, and he whips it at me and misses. I find it brush-side down in the scuzz circling the shower drain.

*

While Vince warms up the engine, I grab the blazer, tie, and button-down from my bag, along with a sweater, get in, and start changing. The windshield's just a couple portholes of defrosted glass, but Vince takes off anyway as soon as I shut my door.

"We're already late—let's grab coffee real quick," I say.

Once he finally feels like talking again, he says, "You're lucky it just so happens that I'm a vegetable without my morning jolt."

We hit up a drive-thru spot down the street. For the first time in memory, Vince actually buys.

We're waiting on our order and I go, "You know what you smell like?"

I see his jaws grind. He twists at the leather steering wheel like he's giving it an Indian burn.

"—A fresh blooming alpine meadow."

I smile and give his shoulder a couple love taps.

Right off the bat, we hit morning rush hour, and Vince lights up in frustration. Before long, we're at a standstill.

"Well, what about the third one?" he says, sighing out smoke.

"Third what?"

"Bachman, Suzette—who's was the third wake?"

"I don't know why I brought all that up," I say, and try the radio.

...traffic and weather together, on the eights, WBBM news radio seventy-eight!

I click it off. "Forgot there's only AM..."

"Finish your story," he says. "Or not. I don't care."

"It's nothing. You don't know him—Vlad Popov. This was back in April. I forget the day. He was just a piano player I knew. Played for ages in St. Petersburg, moved out to Brighton Beach sometime after the Cold War. Him and his two boys. We got to be friends playing this weekly gig at a jazz bar in the village. The owner told me."

"Took the kiddies, left the wife behind, huh. That it?"

"I get to his place out in Brighton pretty late. His son, Peter, answers the door, leads me into the kitchen. But before I sit, before we shake hands, or even take off my jacket, he puts this Dixie cup filled to brimming with vodka in my hands. Says to me, 'The latecomer takes full glass, as penalty.'

"The kitchen gets silent and grim. Everybody watching, making sure I take my penalty. But that stuff was so pristinely distilled, it went down like cold liquefied air. And the liquor was chilled to the point it was viscous, like corn syrup. Couple minutes later, my jaw falls out of my head."

"Russians. When it comes to vodka, they do not kid around."

"He poured another round for everyone. Goes, 'You see, my father was from old country, we have it old country tradition—' His voice cracks; he gets all teary. One man at the table comes over to us, clutches Peter to his chest while he sobs, '—for to honor papochka.'"

"I can respect that. People don't give a fuck about traditions anymore, but without them, we're just, dunno, like—filth."

"They bring out food and we all start porking out on blini. And then drinking more after that. And his other son, Niko, this blubbery mountain in Adidas warmups, who'd been keeping to himself, wolfing down knish and meat dumplings in the corner, practically swallowing them whole. We're in the hall, waiting in line for the bathroom, and he starts talking. I ask him what happened with Vlad. 'It was embolism,' he says to me. 'He inject air in his jugular vein. It is a bad death. In this situation, proper burial, it is not permitted. For this, Peter weeps.'"

"A bad death," Vince says.

"According to Niko, at least."

His face falls.

"Ah, cheer up, Vince. That's just a bunch of superstition. Truth about deaths—they're all bad."

"Okay for real, Ant—seriously, tell me—what is the matter with you?"

"This is getting old, man…"

"Huh? You tell me right now—should I be worried? What're you—robbing graves out there? You need some kind of help? Therapy? I don't understand."

I just gulp down coffee. It's hard to know where to begin certain things.

"*Answer* me," he says, and shoves me in my face.

"You do that again…"

Vince re-grips the wheel. "I will do whatever the hell I like."

He and I go mute. On his side, Vince plays the role of calmest man on earth, but the shaking fingers fumbling for another Camel Gold give him away. On my side, I try to ignore the two kids in the van on my right, who saw it all, but still keep looking.

*

Suzette's funeral wasn't quite as sensational as I let on. I embellished heavily because Vince hates it when I do. If he finds out, of course. Third wife Suzette's funeral saw no food thrown. There was zero charisma from the family members gathered there that day. They were frustrating; it was boring. I left crestfallen, though the coronary did occur. It was while I was on the train back to my apartment that it dawned on me that, after this whole time, it had never crossed my mind to read the obituaries. That made my spirits rise.

As we crawled along with the other cars on the freeway, I start thinking of Charlie Maple, the nothing-memory of him that I learned about in the newspaper.

US Navy. Veteran of the Vietnam War. Made lieutenant after a couple tours in the sopping lowland jungle cloaking the DMZ. This was a couple months before Ray came on the television, before that awful call to Vince.

The notice read: Sunday, between the hours of 11am and 2pm, at which time he will be interred at Green-Wood Cemetery.

To rest among the green woods there, and the green everything else.

It was a soupy late autumn day. Everyone was already graveside when I pulled up, massed around an arthritic tree trunk whose canopy did little to protect them. A dozen or so mourners, the only ones populating the cemetery grounds. The committal was only just underway. I remember wading through the fallen leaves, so many were there, as though coming to shore. Careful to keep a respectful distance, I crept forth, just in time to catch the priest intone: *Death is in your hands...*

Some of the headstones were still lichened and green as limes, stood crooked, like teeth needing braces, or the blunt, cracked thumbnails of an old god in a millennial coma. In a few weeks they'd be frosted, silver shields gleaming in the winter's thin anti-sunlight.

I wanted to observe from afar, unobtrusively, but got nearer to better hear the priest.

...Whoever believes in me shall live even in death and whoever lives and believes in me shall never die.

Maple was a Catholic, a city kid, hurled his purple heart at the feet of the House of Congress in '71, or maybe '72. Then he was a married man, a company man, a father of four daughters full of promise. He had a fall. I overheard a couple lamenting it. He tripped down the subway steps at Fulton Center. His brother insists he was pushed. He must have been his brother, since their faces cracked and creased in the same places about the eyes and nose when he winced through the grief brought less by the priest's words, more by the young daughter of the daughter of the dead lieutenant. I studied the great big photo of his smiling, ecstatic face resting on the easel behind the casket. A face too young to crack so early, but that's war, as the saying goes.

Having endured mortar fire, heavy artillery, guerilla snipers lurking closer every night, fever, leeches, and all sorts of rot and rash of the body, Charlie had a fall, broke his head, could not be put back together again. His final act stopping morning traffic into the city. Maybe that suited him just fine.

...And the hour of death unknown...

I couldn't help admiring the granddaughter playing with her Barbie, as the earthmover loomed behind her, inert, a yellow scorpion of tawdry steel, deep in slumber. The brother holding Charlie's cane, absurdly cradling it in against his chest, as though for protection against all that's out there, as one cradles a rifle, even one prone to inopportune malfunction.

In a fit of boredom and frustration, the granddaughter tossed her doll into the grave before anyone could thwart her, and it was quickly engulfed in soil made the color and consistency of browned, ground chuck by the drizzle. Mother holding back daughter to keep her from rescuing her friend. Tantrum, hard slap that makes everyone's face go red.

"We'll get you a new one on the way home," said mom, mushing the girl's teary face in her grip, then hurrying off in embarrassment and dragging her along.

"But what about *her*?" She pointed a stern finger to where her Barbie had landed. Out of answers and patience, mom just gave a weary sigh, continuing to haul her daughter along while making up an answer that would satisfy.

...Lighten their sense of loss with your presence...

We all focused back on him in the bright, starched white collar and bifocals spotted with rain, despite his hooded slicker.

No one really noticed or seemed to care about my presence at first, so I got closer still, until I was in the center of the horseshoe the others had formed around the earth's open hole.

...Through disobedience to your law we fell from grace and death entered the world...

Gradually, and one by one, the family sensed an imposter. I disregarded their glances, cleared throats, each *ahem* sent my way, until I felt a soft but insistent tap on my shoulder. I didn't turn from the priest. He kept going, reading from his little book. I was enjoying myself.

...at your voice the tombs will open and all the just who sleep in your peace will rise and sing...

"If you're not a friend, I ask that you move on," said a weathered voice near my ear. I imagined that it belonged to an old man, perhaps the father, a war buddy, but I don't know, I didn't bother turning toward it.

Was this what it was like? Wendy, was it at all like this?

...And gently wipe every tear from your eyes...

Thinking of him. Thinking of her. The voice in my ear saying, "Don't make me repeat myself."

I spat in the grass between my feet. The most-lush daffodils flanking either side of the coffin. I resisted the unsettling urge to French kiss each petal, or gobble them down by the handful. I took a step closer. That's when the rifle reports jolted us all out of our skins. It dawned on me I'm the only one in dirty jeans, that I was wearing my Use Your Illusion t-shirt. What I'd slept in. Red flag right there.

Coffee brown birds in a row of scrawny poplars fled after the bang, as though giving chase to the lead rounds bellowing off to heaven. Birds are silly things. The power of flight gives them naive convictions about what's possible.

I turned my attention to the polished bolt action of the rifles as the soldiers reloaded in their impeccable white gloves and awaited the command to fire again, to shatter this moment, like a livid gust slamming shut a storm door.

I never saw the face belonging to the voice. After the third volley split through the quieting air, I wandered away with the others to where I'd parked my car and decided to skip the banquet hall reception. How could I ever tell this to Vince? My hands were trembling as I drove through the gates, and I felt one of the old headaches looming behind my eyes, but my heart was singing out to Charlie; my heart was singing the dead awake.

*

Being one of the last to arrive at Marsden & Goolsby Funeral Services, we park in the nail salon lot across the street and navigate four lanes of traffic and plowed snow to reach the funeral home driveway.

"You know, I just realized—Ray died never knowing—in all likelihood at least—never having experienced a blowjob. And that's kind of sad. He'll never—"

Vin smacks me across the mouth. At first I'm confused. He looks surprised himself.

We're just outside the chapel, off to the side of the building, in the snow between the parked cars and the fire exit. I lunge at him, take him to the ground, where we grapple to a stalemate.

Even at his wedding, except for during the actual ceremony, he'd been on my case about my drinking too early, too hard, even though he was matching me drink for drink. It was maybe sound advice, I admit, but we were warring, in our constant, low-grade way, and when it's like that between people, the line that shall not be crossed is never clear. That was just a week or two before I moved, but here we are, picking up just where we left off.

"Truce?" I say.

Huffing and puffing, Vince shrugs.

We brush dead leaves and snow off our clothes.

"It is a shame, I suppose," he says.

"All I'm saying."

Always bickering, snapping. Just like family. Vince goes in but I stay outside for a minute. I need a calm-down cigarette. This is our united front.

*

At each funeral, there were breakdowns, uncomfortable dead-air moments between myself and strangers attempting to bridge a chasm.

Bachman's daughter swore she'd never forgive her father for catching pneumonia. Vlad's brother swore to me he felt his dead sibling somehow attached to his heart, as if by piano wire, which made it painful to go on the long evening strolls he normally enjoyed. He really said this to me. I couldn't help giggling a bit. He did too, just before falling to pieces. Everything, and everyone—ridiculous.

Just listen and out they come—tragic confessions, vicious little honesties, bitter outpourings spit like pushpins from the mourners' mouths.

I would find something, inevitably. I'd let them off the hook for whatever it was. And I'd return home reassured of my own invincibility and with a wider appreciation for the mysterious ways of creation.

Finishing my smoke, I wander around to the back of the funeral home. As I'm making the corner though, I come across a woman, alone in the rear lot. It takes me a second to register Marcy's face. She looks scrawny and lost, meandering through the landscaping blocking the view of the adjacent homes.

"I just needed some air," she says, when she notices I've seen her.

"Me too."

"You look nice."

"Oh, thanks. Sorry we're late, we just got stuck in traffic."

Marcy is no longer listening, though. She isn't even looking at me.

"Bring him back, Ant. I want him back here. He needs his mom." She brings her fist down lightly on my chest, like she's knocking on a little door, seeing straight through my body.

"I can't, Marcy."

"Bring him back, Ant. I'm going mad."

I shake my head at this. "I don't know how."

Marcy nods at me, though it's all a confused front, all hurt, as though English were now unfathomable to her. But she remains there, knocking clumps of snow from a spruce tree limb. The dust glitters around her. I wipe my eyes. I have to leave. I suddenly need to be closer to the warmth of the living.

*

Father Devin Leper talks with a certain tick; it makes him nervously yank on his shirt collar, as if it were too snug around the neck. He introduces himself and offers me his bony hand.

"I'm a friend of the family," I say.

"Please, most everyone has assembled in our visitation chapel, if you'll follow me. Did the Channel 9 news crew arrive yet?"

"I don't know anything about that."

"They said they would come. Then again, they always say that…"

We head into the short, wide hall, where a crowd mingles. I clear my throat as we approach, and nod at those faces

I recognize. Father Leper, tall and gaunt, floats throughout the room, expressing his sympathies again and again.

Vince leans against a Steinway in the corner. I'm slowly making the rounds, embracing relatives, shaking hands with friends, and avoiding introductions with the few I've never seen before.

"What can you say about these freak accidents?" cousin Patricia says to me. She nibbles at the square of coffee cake she's got loosely wrapped in a napkin. I give her question some thought.

"Nothing," I say. "You can't say anything, really."

"And yet—I have to. We all have to keep on saying these empty, meaningless things to each other."

Vince's Uncle Miles says to her, "They ought to ban ownership of the breed. They shouldn't be kept as pets. I'll say that much. Get a lab. Get a poodle."

Patricia glances at him, listening, but makes no reply. Angling it so it fits, she negotiates the rest of the pastry into her mouth.

I make my way to the back of the line formed to pass Ray's casket when Marcy appears at the chapel doors like an outlaw with unfinished business at a saloon. The withering stare she casts about the room seems a dare to stop her. As it falls upon the faces of all her loved ones, less loved now, they wilt. But there is no acknowledgment in her eyes, nothing registers, moving as though the place was vacant.

How many times had I seen that look? It was only the little kids that got it, after taking a basketball to the face some big kid chucked at them, after being pantsed in front of everyone, after someone claimed carnal knowledge of their mother, and they storm over to the big kid, the last straw crushed in their fists, and they confuse rage for the ability to fight. Had those looks ever led to anything good? I don't think I ever stuck around to witness the massacre.

Shouldering her way through the crowd, no one here would like anything more than to make way.

Dan's behind her then, fishing for her hand through the other limbs pressing around her, saying, "C'mon, Marce," in a whisper, "C'mon now, Marcy, I know. Let's keep it together, for our boy."

But she's already before the coffin, caressing the shellacked surface. He is afraid of touching her. I see him thinking twice—hand floating inches above her arm, her waist, her right shoulder blade, as though unstable fields of psychic energy would dissolve whatever fingers made contact.

She has obliterated the line. Guests scatter for open seats, or clear stretches of wall. Briefly, the room is silent. I can hear Marcy's long blue nails, clicking like talons along the coffin's spotless lid, as she gazes down at her boy's form, even though it's closed. I see the fingerprints she leaves there too, after Dan pulls her away.

"It's what you wanted, remember?" he says. "Vin, we need some help up front. Ant? Heck are you doing here…"

Vince shrugs my way as Dan drags him off to Marcy, sulking against the staircase, walled off by blushing pallbearers.

I trail them down the hall, silent for the carpet, though Dan's priority seems to be speed rather than discretion. At the far end of the hall there's a left, and at the top of a five-step staircase, a kind of lounge or break room that seems meant for next of kin. I stay at the bottom, close enough to hear, standing against the wall by a pedestal displaying a marble bust of some woman with ridiculous hair. I can see three or so pairs of legs arranged around those of a wooden table.

"You'll feel better," Dan says. "I'm just trying to help you get through this."

"That's very sensible of you, Daniel. You're so rational."

"Honey—I don't—it hurts me to see you like this."

She gasps, "Oh, I've *embarrassed* you."

"Vince—"

"I've ruined this for you, haven't I. This isn't how it was supposed to *go*. You had—let me guess—a *vision* for the *look* of your son's wake and I've bent that *all* out of *shape*."

"Goddamn it. Vince, give 'em here."

"Good boy, Vince."

"Thank you, Vince. I'm sorry. You can get back there. We'll talk later."

I see Vince stand, back up from the table. What I hear is sort of slurred but really, unmistakable—Marcy struggling. Her mouth sounds covered. Marcy coughing, retching. Dan's prudent, good-doctor's voice, telling her to swallow, saying it's for the best, it's supposed to help.

Vin busts me eavesdropping as he comes down the stairs, taking two at a time. But he doesn't say a word, just strides into the back doors like the Incredible Hulk, everything fine and just jim-dandy, right past Father Leper, who is just outside, still holding out hope for Channel 9 to show.

*

I follow him out to the four-lane road, but miss the light and have to wait. Everything is lights and waiting around to cross crosswalks in this dump. Everything is timing. Vince fronts like he doesn't see I'm right here.

"Gonna ditch me?" I yell.

But Vince unlocks the car and gets in. I cross when the light's finally green again. Going casually, as if doing so rendered the threat of being marooned here preposterous, even though it's not. I've ditched him before. He's ditched me. Those days were long ago, those betrayals petty, only devised to give the feeling we were gangsters fleeing a job gone south, or to see the other in dire straits for a second.

However, whether desertion in the wastes of suburban Wisconsin is or was ever on the table, Vince's still idling in the Cutlass when I reach him there. He even lets me get in.

"The ground is too hard for burial, this deep into winter," I say, and light a cigarette. "Using the backhoe can seem callous, unless requested by the bereaved. Same for the jackhammer. If this place has the facilities, perhaps a grave-thawer, it may not be an issue. Whether Dan and Marcy plan to cremate, or simply wait for spring, I don't know. Dan looks to be handling it pretty well though…"

"That's Dan for you, isn't it," Vince says.

"What's he again? A anesthesiologist?"

"Real estate broker."

"Could've told them I was coming…"

Vince puts us in reverse and backs out. "It slipped my mind, Ant. Not everything's about you…"

"Where to now? Another errand to run? Off to the pharmacy, I mean cemetery? Which is which, I can't tell anymore."

"Don't you have a plane to catch or something? Thought you were done here. What you want to head back to Ray's place for? Need a kielbasa fix?"

"I've got time yet."

"Oh, come *on*." He stomps on the brakes. The force jerks the car.

"Hey, at least the brakes work."

Vince puts us in park and lifts his bandaged hand. "See this? Well guess what, Ant. It hurt. And guess what else, it still fucking hurts." Vince unvelcros the straps of the neoprene brace with a trembling hand and chucks it on the dash. The gauze beneath it has gone maroon in splotches.

"You could use a change."

"Me and everyone else." Wheezing out in pain, he peels off the sticky strips clinging to his wrist. His breath puffs out in the frosted afternoon light.

Underneath, Vince's hand is distended and unclean, mushroom blue about the knuckles, sutures protruding like a line of thick black in-grown hairs. "Turns out when you punch a concrete column as hard as you can, the concrete wins. There was a bolt screwing the sign in place, a fat son of a gun, and gave me these cuts.

"Now pay attention, Ant, it gets complicated—you punch a concrete column and bust up your shit, and what they do nowadays is when you do that shit, the doctor gives you a bunch of little magic pills that kill the pain. Just like that, old buddy. So quit looking at me like I'm some kind of fucking—Jack the Ripper or whatever."

I do as he says, watching while he redresses the wound.

"...You could've just told me. Didn't need to see it. And that whole 'I hammered my hand' thing?"

"You know I could probably hammer nails blindfolded by now. Anything else, officer? Or can we go?"

"Give me one and we're cool. You been holding out on me."

"God, you're a vulture."

"You ruined my funeral," I say.

He groans, then yelps. He wrapped the gauze too tight.

"...Bottle's in my coat."

I reach in the backseat, grab at his sport coat.

"Not the blazer," he says, "the p-parka."

I find the clear orange bottle in the inside pocket, give it a little rattle, and pop it open.

"He payin' you? For the pills?"

"Not a lot of work for a roofer in the winter. Those're thirties, now," Vince tells me, shifting in his seat, "take just a half."

"The better half, right?"

"Well. I guess that all depends on how your day is going," he says, and helps himself to one as well.

*

To our right, the sun is a hurt red drain. For a long time I don't know how to talk to him. Maybe it was the oxy. Maybe it was Ray, who will be kept in a drawer until April, or maybe seeing Marcy, lost in herself and lost in the snow. There is a woozy half hour of driving, of fuzz-sunk warmth, knotted to nausea, cold sweat, before I hit a kind of blithe cruising altitude.

Crossing back into Illinois, to Dan and Marcy's, landmarks dredge up old states of mind, childish, idle daydreams, but I just smirk at them, too fried to feel much. That drain in the sky draws us toward it, toward the wide, river-split ravine along which, long ago, limestone was hewn free by the ton and used to build Chicago.

Vince blows his nose in a McDonald's napkin and murmurs, "Think I should get off the road."

"You are such a total pussy, Vince, I swear."

"Should probably eat something. Not worth—crashing…"

So I turn to him. I look at Vince, at Vince's weirdly downy freckled earlobe. He keeps his face forward, pretending I don't exist, but I know he feels it. I think he feels it, at least. He hiccups. We accelerate.

"Today the day?" he asks, letting go.

The wheel, once it's free, turns by itself.

"All right, all right, Christ almighty, you win."

Vince pulls the wheel his way, steers us true, and I get wracked with electric shivers of delight, nape to tailbone, as we swirl down the exit like a wind-caught feather to the Funny Bunny nestled underneath the overpass.

"Can you believe it's barely past four pm?" Vince says, gazing up at intestinal clouds the color of old tangled shoelaces that the winds seem keen to rip apart.

"I believe I can."

We have a grim chuckle, commiserating, for a moment, in this shared plight. It's ours. It's all we sometimes have. Smiling as we purchase our stupid glazed donuts, a dozen of them, laughing as we force each one, all warm and shiny with icing, into our numb mouths, as we swallow down, our tongues barely tasting a thing, but what they make out tasting superb enough to wash out almost everything about today. By the time we reach the car, though, even that is fading, draining fast as rain-drenched sidewalk chalk.

A snowflake, two, floating heavy and aimless as cottonwood seeds between us. Then more. I hold out my hand. I want the car keys, but Vince, the box of donuts under his arm, the keychain dangling from his mouth, just gives me a firm handshake.

We get in and without much thought at all the both of us wipe our hands on the seats—streaks of sugar and soot. Old habits die hard. And so we split another pill, partially as a compromise, and since we are unable to come up with a single damn reason why it ought not be like this all the time, and we peel out, and Vince even pulls a run of radical donuts in the parking lot, burning rubber through sloppy snow, the few customers inside watching with dread, and I'm laughing and dizzy as we book out of there like hell-raisers, leaving what would be the last of the light far behind us, and Vince is laughing, but with tears bright as chrome running down to his chin when the lights hit them, another thing we can barely metabolize, much less talk about.

*

Dan and Marcy's house isn't terribly far away, but we speed the whole way down, since the roads are miraculously clear as they've been all weekend. There are cars parked up and down the snow-banked cul-de-sac when we get there. Vince bends a couple fenders parking. I ring the buzzer, but he snorts, "Just go on in."

Dan's just about to open the door when we walk up. The place is crammed with people.

The Christmas tree's still up. Someone's kids are playing tag with somebody's cousins. Dan shakes my hand. It sobers me up a little.

"Long time no see," I say. He grimaces, a tacit acknowledgement of the scene back at the funeral home. I look around for Vince but he's already melted away.

"You caught us by surprise back there," he says, and though I have some clever remark all loaded up, I just squeeze his arm. By this, I hope he knows I know tough days can go sideways on people, that whatever it was I saw back there won't be held against him. I'm not sure what else to do, nor am I sure whether Dan expects a different sort of performance of grief. I don't ask about Marcy.

"The roads are pretty clear," I say, taking off my coat.

"Yeah, they're good about plowing," Dan says. "From I-80 all the way up to Northville, they're running the salt trucks. We'll see how long that lasts. Weather says we're supposed to get a bit more snow tonight."

"Traffic was great, I was shocked."

"Marcy and I just flew down. I was worried, with all that construction they got going on, over in... what's that place. Not Kenosha..." Dan's snapping his fingers.

"Algonquin?"

"Over there in Waukegan. They got that expansion on the 94 that they're doing. It's down to one lane all winter."

"Gross."

"Just a mess. Used to go skating out there. They had a rink off the edge of the lake, you could take the kids."

"That sounds nice. We had that little pond out by us."

"I remember."

"You see where Vince snuck off to?"

"He's not with you?"

"No, he was, I just—

"Personally, I never liked ice skating."

It could have been any Christmas Eve family get-together, the way the old banter played itself out between us, I think. Automatic as a player piano. Dan was aching for it, and the thought brings a little shudder. His family was destroyed and Dan wants to schmooze. I excuse myself then, having spotted the wet bar in the parlor, wondering: and am I so different?

I grab a short clear plastic cup from the stack and pour a vodka, but it's too well distilled. I want my throat torched. How did we come to believe employing such poor, impulsive tactics would convince us that things, that we, are under control? Just how many holes can one man dig? As we both meekly fall back to opposite corners of the room, I can't help pondering this bewilderment: perhaps I should've cracked him in the jaw, maybe he should've spat in my mouth?

Everyone revisits the old memories, staring at the cold cuts, tuna casserole, mostaccioli, waiting for the food line to dwindle.

Some may find this sad, or pathetic. I certainly did, for the lion's share of my youth and young adulthood, but I don't really, anymore. And though the conversation is a little boring, a little shallow, a little bit grating, how they are, how they have been, what they are going or have been through—a bit of authenticity does shine through the rote, typical small talk we make as the mushroom soup is ladled out and bowls are passed around.

The sour Midwestern accents have deepened and calcified in their throats, their words now short a syllable here and there. The old grudges too, which I have been largely absent for, are more entrenched, now tribal lore; the weary, inflected anger when griping on homeowners associations, the stubborn stances on Mayor Daley now taken for gospel, for essential wisdom, the way they rave about the latest Michael Bay blockbuster—it's just variations on a theme. What we say never changes. How we say it reveals our age, a history invisible to the stranger's eye, one that is never really addressed by those familiar with it.

What I reveal of myself in my blasé non-answers remains beyond me, as theirs are to them. Whether this is sad I can't say, but it endears me to this messy band of suburban dead-enders, for a moment.

I'm trying to unpack all of this to Kristen, four, the niece of Caroline's sister Elisa, I think. I'm sitting on the stairs as she comes dragging a puff plastic tricycle down the steps. But after a minute of listening, she tells me she's gotta run, I'm super boring, and rides her plastic trike through the orchard of legs to the fridge for a grape Crush, her favorite.

She parks her ride against my knee and asks me to open her can of soda, climbing into my lap with a Ziploc of crayons and a coloring book. By now, those pills are in full bloom.

"What's that you got?" I ask.

"Colors."

"Oh, nice. What color's roses?"

"Red."

"Very good. What about grass?"

"Mmm... brown. Is Ray really dead?"

"Pretty sure he is."

"Where do people go when they die?"

"The airport. I want a sip of soda."

"I'm outta here," she says, and gets back on her tricycle, turning imaginary keys. I give her ride a little kick and off she goes, running over feet toward the TV room.

*

"There is little to report about me—work is fine, life is fine, it feels good being back!" This is what I tell the others—Auntie Irene and her glum posse of Old World Polskis, seated knee-to-knee around the sectional sofa, as though guarding their monopoly on the crudité platter no one wants. Each grumbles a weary reply, but I can tell they don't expect more news than this. Each gets a peck on the cheek, then I'm craving a smoke, a breather, rushing to slip outside, but Dan flags me down from across the room and makes his way over.

"Watch yourself," he says. "Our back deck's been invaded by gremlins."

I open the sliding door and clusters of beady eyes peer at me. Huffys, Schwinns, all piled up in the yard like fuel for a bonfire.

Ray's high school classmates. Wouldn't venture to call them friends, but what do I know about Ray, the high school freshman?

Out on the deck everyone's coifed and dressed for confirmation—all sweater vests and oxford shirts underneath parkas, in hand-me-down loafers. A few booze and share smokes around the table, playing stud poker in winter gloves. Others are out back, got a game of drunk horse going in the drive.

The boys' cheeks are raw from razor burn. Braces glint when some of them grin.

The girls shiver in wool skirts and mall jewelry. They all squint my way. I'm just a silhouette made from the kitchen light.

A scan of their faces is all it takes to confirm I don't know any of them, do not really want to, that Vin's not here, and that *gremlins* is the perfect word for them.

When I turn to leave, someone shouts my name. He is hard to find at first.

"Lo and Behold, is that an Ant I spy?"

They watch me. Some take a step or two closer.

"What's the good word?" He gives a light toss of his keychain, with its red rabbit's foot, and snatches it from the air, watching me.

"Oh, nothing much."

They all bob their heads, sip their Solo cups. Some return to arguing Illini football. One big-eared boy fake trips on his shoelace and tries groping either of the two girls nearby.

"*Randall*, ugh…"

"Think they're gonna you know—burn him?"

"Seen Vince?"

"Maybe," says the guy who knows me but whose name I don't know, though I dub him Bat Neck, on account of the blue vampire bat tattoo sprawling across the width of his throat. "He was on the phone with someone inside someplace."

His eyes flash blue as wiper fluid when I trigger the security lights on my way back in. He's been out of school a decade at least.

"Marcy and Dan are laying him to rest after winter," I mention.

"Wait up." He drops his Newport in the frozen pot of geraniums on the table. "Let's get a quick game in first. Hey, you guys, clear the table. Mumbly-peg, lightning round."

The kids come to life and crowd around. Ten, maybe fifteen of them, sopping up most of the light given from the twin bulbs screwed into the eaves.

"...Probably not drunk enough yet," I say, as Bat Neck splays his left hand atop the table.

Before he begins, he lets me see the blade of his survival knife, holds it up close to my face and at such an angle the black metal's sharpened edge catches the light beams and flashes its thin silver half-smile.

"He bested me last time. I got a good memory," he says, tapping his temple. Then looking at the others. A few are wiping their runny noses on their sweater sleeves. One tall, snickering beanstalk of a kid is taking a steaming piss in the bird bath. "I got good aim now though," he says, spinning that ring of keys on his finger like a gunslinger.

"I'm sure you do."

"C'mon, Ant, I'm kidding. Don't be a bitch. Ray's watching."

"Lord Jesus too," one of them says, then the others start smelling fear and giggle and echo the call—"*C'mon, PLAY for RAY.*"

"Yeah, Ant, play for Ray, may he rest in peace. Chuckie, hit him with a swig first." Bat Neck sits up. His splayed-finger hand hasn't moved since he first placed it down flush like a sticker before him. Chuckie passes me his bottle of Jäger. It's heavy, tastes black as it looks, makes me sputter.

Bat Neck starts. The knife hops between his thumb and index with increasing speed, then leaps back, maintaining pace, then goes back again, and from there into the next gap, between his ring and middle fingers. He's jabbing the tabletop like mad now. Everyone is silent. Back goes the blade, and it repeats its hopscotch, to the last space between his fingers, when he says, "What you got, Ant?" and pushes his speed. Little gougings mar the plastic. Close little groupings. The others are hypnotized.

"Okay now, dinner's getting cold," croaks Auntie Irene from the sliding doorway, and all the kids glare at her, even Bat Neck, whose blade then cuts into his thumb's webbing. It yawns wide open, a small red mouth, before beginning to bleed everywhere, and Auntie Irene makes a quick retreat inside again.

He puts the wound to his mouth. The girl in the bright yellow puffy coat hurls a wad of napkins at him and averts her eyes. A sick mirth spreads amongst them all. Bat Neck's laughing too then.

"Your go," he says, then he's sucking at the cut and rubbing out the blood drops with his sneaker.

"After dinner."

Groans and boos from all around. Someone whips a crushed empty at me, then runs away. Quick ripple of *oohs* and *ahs*.

Down on the back lawn the smallest, goofiest one pours his drink all over his buddy who said something, soaking him in blue punch and sending him to the ground in a fit of laughter.

"I *told* you this'd be awesome…" a girl says to her pal.

"Nah, see, he's a pussy, just like Ray," he says.

"Dog food," someone mutters, a scrawny misfit late to arrive, hopping up and down to keep the blood pumping, not sure what's going on. Another leers at me and Bat Neck like it's a peep show.

I sit down at the table. Bat Neck licks the flat of the blade and makes a girl shudder.

I make a half dozen stabs before slashing a knuckle. The crowd cheers, but it's short-lived when they see I'm not embarrassed or at all concerned by the cut. From the kitchen window, Auntie Irene glowers, draws the little curtain when our eyes meet.

I shrug. I sit there, let the flesh wound drip as the mob melts away, hunts for something new to tantalize them, a few of the boys gobbling down hot roast beef sandwiches taken from the kitchen.

"You're not as fun as I remember," Bat Neck says to me, and juts out his lower lip in a mock sad face.

"You're about the same," I reply. Whoever he really is, there were many just like him back in school. They were churned out by the dozen.

Standing then, I lean in to give him a couple rough pats on the cheek, and before he can pick up his blade, I swipe up his dumb keys and chuck them as far as I can into the dark beyond the wood fence at the end of the property, then make my way indoors.

I'm not as fast or accurate as Bat Neck. But I'm not afraid of knives. Mom taught me that.

*

Evelyn, Vince's mom, is smoking with Marcy in the upstairs bedroom when I come up looking for him. Except for the soft glow of a night-light plugged in the socket by their feet, the two quietly sit together in weak shadow.

Evelyn fans away the cloud she exhales, saying when she sees me, "It's all right, it's okay—I got the ceiling fan goin'. Don't go tattlin' on us." Gingerly, Evelyn rises and embraces me, the cool aunt I never had. She's frail in my arms now, smaller than I recall, wearing glasses with thicker lenses, but her sarcastic sense of humor has only appreciated with time. I've missed her more than I thought.

Marcy sniffs, tries out a laugh. "Come, sit with us, Ant," she says, patting Ray's bed.

Here I am, in his bedroom, with its White Sox pennant, Slayer poster, cracked digital clock on the wall. I'm already ready to leave. Downstairs, I can hear guests are starting to give their goodbyes. This room is rank with dryer sheets and the dull sting of Calvin Klein cologne.

"He was such a good boy," says Marcy.

"It's all beyond me," I say. "Dogs don't know any better. Their behavior's a reflection of their training. Maybe Gavin will get what's coming to him one of these days. Hopefully, who knows."

"I meant Ray," Marcy says.

"We could give a darn about the dog..." Evelyn adds.

Marcy shakes her head at me. "Bullets was not put down. He got loose."

"I guess Vin never said specifically. I just assumed the cops had him in the pound."

"It's only a matter of time. Certainly by tomorrow. They'll get him," Marcy says.

"Where *is* Vin, by the way? He disappeared the minute we got in."

"You know how he is," Evelyn says. "Crowds make him pan-icky." She rolls her eyes, and that cracks me up a little bit. Marcy gives a dreamy smile.

I get up from the bed. "I should go find him. I have to fly back tonight," I say. "You want a light on?"

Marcy shakes her head. "I'm fine like this. My eyes are just so *sore*..."

"Good seeing you, Ant," Evelyn says, leaning over, gripping my arm. "Now, if you don't see him downstairs, try the Jawarski's. He's there all the time. We're not *fun* enough for him anymore, I suppose."

She moves to the rocking chair in the corner. Marcy says, "If you find him though, send him here. He's got something I need." Evelyn nods, gives her trembling hand a squeeze of support.

*

I wander down a silent, fresh-plowed lane, through the murk and Christmas lights hung from the alley gutters. Above them, the night sky is a dead television screen.

The Jawarskis were like a clan. Four or five brothers, couple sisters between them, each terrorizing us all in their own ways. They all ought to be grown and busy forming their own little broods by now.

The Jawarski home has the same drab-cream clapboard siding, that same ramshackle screen door that always thwacked me. I remember I never liked that house. But I was buds with Melvin for about a year back in junior high. He was second oldest of the litter. Until he turned on me that fall, I had a kind of immunity against their cruelty, or at least the worst manifestations of it. One of their favorite games was chasing unpopular kids up trees. Whoever kept them up there after nightfall won a point.

A rough gust rollercoasters just overhead, brings a dive bomb shriek like squealing children, then vanishes, a rogue wave I'm glad to have missed. The homes groan back into place, the cellophaned windows quit their rattle.

Vince is huddled in the little vestibule in front of their place, struggling to undo a cufflink as he waits to be let in.

"Oh, Christ. Buzz off, Ant."

"Oh, hi, Vincent. What brings you here…"

"Why don't you just go back to the house and I'll catch up with you later?" He rips the sleeve open. "Hate these buttons…"

"There's the Vince I know and love."

"Get your head checked."

The eyeball peeking past the deadbolt chain belongs to Mrs. Jawarski, I assume, but the gates swing open upon sight of Vince.

"*Vinnie.* How are *you*! C'mere. Hugs. I can't *tell* you how *sorry* we are, ugh, it's just god awful—come in, and who's—?"

"This is Ant, my old neighbor."

"*Ant.* Sure, I remember. You're *back*. How've you *been*, oh, you get hugs too," she says, coming in close. "I'm Margaret," she adds.

So, okay.

A *Friends* re-run is on in the living room.

"Should we take our shoes off?" I ask.

"They don't care about that," Vince says.

"Sure, if you like," she replies.

"We won't be long, Mrs. Jawarski. I just came to meet up with Daymon," he says.

"He's out back in the garage since yesterday."

"What's he doing?" I ask, but Mrs. Jawarski just throws her hands in the air, shuffles into the pantry.

"Stop. Talking," Vince says.

"So, Ant, what do you do for a living?" she calls.

I look to Vince. "Should I answer?" He only sucks his cheek and stares at the mottled off-white carpeting. There's a little wild-haired Pomeranian eyeing me from a doorway down the hall.

"Why hello, Roxy!" she says. I hear her make smooching noises, but Roxy stays put. "Now—would either of you like a slice of pie? I got key lime," she calls.

"None for me. I'm on medication," I say, as Vince, with a stealth uncommon for him, sneaks toward the side door, fully cognizant of each creak in the floor and stepping around them. "I just had a—root canal."

"Ugh," Mrs. Jawarski says. "Terrible. I hope they gave you some good dope."

"A little too good."

She returns to the living room, carrying a wedge of key lime pie with a black plastic spoon stuck under it like a shovel.

"I want your dentist," she says, and lowers herself into the Barcalounger in the corner, the plate and TV clicker in either hand, as though to show off the 8-bit Rudolph printed on her sweatshirt.

"Vince run off already?"

"I'll go find him. Think he went out back."

"Good luck with that. Oh, but do me a favor—tell my darling son to lower the volume on that goddamn stereo already. He's had it on all day."

I slip into the side alleyway leading behind the house, unhook the chain-link gate. Vince hears it squeak shut and scowls at me.

They have a backyard path of stone slabs arranged so that visitors can use it and not trample the lawn when going to the garage. But the grass is mostly frozen dirt now, and the stones only get about halfway to the garage before they sink too deep into the earth to be any good. Neither of us bother with it. Even were it not beyond saving, I get the sense that trampling on some withered Kentucky bluegrass is the least of our troubles.

There is a bastard noise bleeding out from behind the garage door. Like a dirt bike raping a leopard.

Vince bangs to be let in. I remember where I am and how little lawns matter. When I hear the barking, it all comes together.

"You punched a column. You hammered your hand. 'Stupid of me.'"

The rattle of padlocks unlatching, the clamor of chains pulled free.

"Hell is this, Vince...?"

He turns to me, we're nose-to-nose. Starts pointing his finger.

"You *shoosh* up now. And get inside with me. You're up in my business."

"Got the rabies shot, right?"

The garage door rises in a loud rush and I'm blinded by this rack of halogen floodlights aimed outward from the back corners, see a brilliant X after shutting my eyes. We freeze like caught burglars. But it's just a kid voice rasping out behind the too-bright glare.

"I blanked man, sorry. My bad. Come on in."

By then, it doesn't really matter whether my eyes adjust, or whether I want them to.

*

Daymon brings the door down after us. He's got the boombox on, some ghastly band, all brutal shrieks strafing over pounding sludge, too loud for the speakers pumping it out, but Daymon isn't bothered, looking at us staring at the blood pattern on the cement floor. He falls back into his folding chair, smooths down his blond buzz cut.

"What's with the blood, Daymon?" Vince says.

"How old are you?" I ask.

He's nodding along to the noise, lazily untangling some jumper cables running along his workstation. A lawnmower is tarped in one corner, a few shelves sag with power tools, a weed-whacker, spare parts. A full-size fridge sits in the other corner, and next to it, that soot-dusted stereo, a pile of garden hoses, the trash cans, and lastly, a big old box, draped by a Garfield beach towel.

"I'm seventeen-and-a-half," he says, picking at a rash along his upper lip and around his nostrils.

"How's your brother, Melvin?"

"Melvin's... Melvin, man, he don't change..."

"It in there?" Vince says. When he doesn't respond, Vince claps his hands at him. "Hey. Daymon. Bit of friendly advice: lay off the paint thinner. Better off sucking a muffler. What happened here?"

I'm just staring at the box in the corner. "Why is there blood all over the place."

"Sorry about the loud music. Keeps snoops away. I'm over these doom and gloom bummer jams," he says, looking where we look. "And anyway, he's quiet now."

When Daymon cuts the sound I snap out of it. "This what you do now, Vin? Torture pets with the local teen psycho? *I* have problems?"

Daymon makes a move toward me, nimble and woozy motion, gets me in a half-nelson, like I'm twelve again. I didn't see it coming. The strength of his hold jogs my memory of his brother, Carlo, the particular Jawarski bozo who tormented my class.

When I don't put up a fight, he loses interest. Letting me go, he says, "It's not nice to make fun of others. Dumb doctors are getting so stingy with painkillers. Dentists aren't bad though. They like, sympathize with people in pain."

He reaches into his mouth and roots around, extracts a set of upper dentures, gleaming with drool, and places it onto the Garfield towel. He does the same with the lower set, dropping it beside its partner. Then, like a viper, he bares his ruined gums at me. Only has a couple molars left.

"I'm not embarrassed either. It was worth a prescription." Daymon casually wipes clean each set with the towel as he talks. "We're all works in progress, Pop says. I am what I am. I know other guys that've done a *whole* lot worse. Girls too."

Vince's still transfixed by that box. He creeps toward it, kneels, then pauses.

"How're you gonna do it?" Daymon says.

Vince lifts the towel. When he murmurs, "I'm slaughtering it," his gaze strays not one inch from what he sees inside.

Daymon presses something into his hand, does the same to me.

"I had a idea, for like—a necklace. Be kind of like dog tags. Eye for an eye, tooth for a tooth. You know what I mean? Bullets too, now. Him and me are like brothers, now."

The dry fang feels warm in my hand, sharpest where it broke. My flight leaves in two and a half hours.

*

Vince isn't listening anymore. The kennel has him slack-jawed, draws his focus into its confines.

"I hate it. He was my bud, you know? We were friends," Vince says. "I can't stop squirming. That sounds weird. I know. It would to me, if one of you said it. I don't care."

"And such a fricking goof too. Dang—I'm making myself cry over here," Daymon says. He lets out a deep breath. "This'll make things right, Vino."

"Nah… no, it won't. It won't right much. But that's—what is that, Ant?—that's immaterial. When disaster strikes. What do we do? We adjust the protocols. Close loopholes. Revise the response. Fix it good. So it can't happen again," Vince murmurs, tapping the kennel bars.

I watch as Daymon, nodding along to Vince's shady wisdom, unscrews the cap off the red gasoline tank by the mower. He stuffs a dishrag down the neck and upends it, sloshes it around. Wringing out the cloth, he then clamps it over his nose and mouth, and his eyes roll back as he sucks in deep. I watch Daymon swoon, one hand blind-groping for the chair he tumbles into once it's felt. His body slackens. It twitches one or two times.

I clear my throat, say, "Cops'll put down Bullets, you know. They'll close the loophole—"

"Quiet now, Ant."

"Not like they're gonna give the dog *parole*—"

"You *still* think I can't handle my own. Call the cops, if you think that's best. Go on." He folds his hands, twiddles his thumbs, waiting. "Well?"

Outside, frustrated gusts rush and batter the metal garage door, demanding entry, as though they too sought shelter from elements of nature more dangerous than them.

Vince stirs, looks for his coat, then swipes the saw hung from a nail in the wall. "I'm taking your hack," he says to Daymon, who is just now coming-to.

"…Think I'm gonna hang back, man. I don't feel too good. Pretty sure Bullets took to it though. Dog's tough," Daymon says with a smile that collapses. He takes up his false teeth and struggles to fit them back in his jaw the right way.

"You're unbelievable," I say to Vince, who *tsks* and says, "Just get the car. Wouldn't want you to miss your flight." He lobs me his keys.

Mrs. Jawarski scrapes plates of some slop that looks like beef stroganoff into the trash outside and sees me bee-lining it to Vince's car.

"What's going on back there?" she calls.

I pretend I don't hear, cutting back into the alley, jogging now to where we parked.

She comes down the deck steps into the yard, rewrapping her robe against the chill. I peer down the street at her watching me in front of the Cutlass. But there is a big problem. The keys aren't fitting. The lock's frozen solid.

"I *said*, what's going on back there?" Mrs. Jawarski is next to me all of a sudden, poking me in the ribs.

"Oh, nothing," I tell her. "Dude stuff, you know."

She frowns. "Oh, *nothing*," she parrots.

But I can smell the liquor on her breath. "I mean, they sent me to grab some booze down the street. But, look: the lock seems to be frozen!"

She squints at me, then the handle. "Gimme the keys. Let me try." Handing them to her, she starts to fiddle.

Call the police. It's there, right there on my tongue. Say it.

"Ugh. Come on. Some whisky should do the trick." Taking me by the hand, she leads me back to her house.

*

From the living room's bay window, they could almost be snow-globe figurines, Vince and Bullets, out back in the moon's sorry milk, were it not for the pillowcase covering the pitbull's head. Sighting me, he taps the wristwatch he isn't wearing.

Mrs. Jawarski pours Wild Turkey into a saucepan over the bathroom sink. Takes a glug herself before handing it over to me. "Wait a minute," she says. "Why not just take the bottle? Save you boys a trip."

I'm already making for the door. "Oh that's all right," I say, balancing the pan of booze. "I think it'd be... a violation of our party ethics."

"Nonsense, here, just wait one second..."

At that, a flagstone crashes in through the window. Glass flies in a lethal dazzle. Roxy goes berserk. The room's heat is outmuscled, snuffed by a ludicrous, swirling cold that renders it condemned, defiled—not a home. I take off by instinct.

I'm running up the street as fast as I can without the saucepan splashing too much, not daring to look back. Everything is moving too fast, too too fast now. I'm thinking *this is bad*, I'm thinking *what the hell am I doing?* as I run, as first one, then three neighbors' porches brighten, as a few watch me in their windows, phones in hand, and I'm breathless, and the answer refraining in my mind: *I do not know.*

The spill of whisky down the door makes the lock steam and softly hiss in the night. I pour some on the key too, and it works. The frozen door cracks free like ice from a tray. Fingers sticky with liquor, I get the car started and head 'round the block to the back alley, where Vince has the dog in a tight grip, slung over his shoulder.

"What the *fuck* was that?" I yell at him.

"You can't do anything right. Not even the simplest thing."

Vince and I get Bullets into the trunk. Another coughing fit seizes him, this one worse than the others, makes him double over.

Mrs. Jawarski is out in front of the sedan, flushed and frenetic in the headlights. "Who did that? I mean, god forbid, could've been killed—*now* what am I supposed to do?"

"Terrible, thoughtless," Vince says. "Probably some teens. Go on in and call the police, though who knows if they'll even come…"

"I just called 'em."

"I can tarp up the frame tonight and get someone to replace it tomorrow."

"I'm *cold*."

"Daymon's got a space heater."

"Vincent, *you* threw it." She is quivering and she is truly cross. Roxy is growling on the deck, bearing thumbtack fangs. And here come the neighbors, trudging forth over the snow-laden pavement in their heavy coats, slow as spacemen.

"Go back inside, Mrs. Jawarski, I'm tellin' ya. They might still be out there."

I close the trunk carefully but that feels pointless now, with those words of his from before burrowing into my mind— *Contusions of the lung. Contusions of the heart.*

*

I know the place we're going. It used to be a Girl Scout camp, then it burned down. Now the woods have taken over. The street degrades into potholes and blacktop chunks buckled by road salt and relentless wild grass. Just on the other side of the car door, dead flutes, blown by a raving band of currents, until Vince kills the engine, and they rest, as though some nonsense game of hide and seek were being played, whose rules changed at whim.

For a moment, all is still. The night is clear and sharpened by frozen air, the moon wide awake, as pocked and cratered as the paving. But the blue-silver clouds are carving through the sky with a haste that just looks off.

Vince parks near a railroad tie and a metal NO ENTRY sign on a chain, hung to keep vehicles out of the lifeless meadow spreading out into the snowy forest.

Vince elbows my shoulder and we go around to get the dog. Given the quiet of the woods, the gray farmland hiding, in its ripple, a silo here, a barn husk over there, it's weird to know we aren't more than a couple miles from home. On the horizon, I can see I-94, glittering pale gold.

"Shattered mouth or no, if we don't pay attention, one of us may lose a valued piece of our anatomy when we open that trunk," he says.

"We could just leave him in there, let nature take its course."

Vince just shakes his head.

"We could leave him in there, go grab a beer. Booze and pills, is nothing better?"

But he isn't having that. Vince wants to count down from three. We'll pop it then, but when he does, and the trunk springs up, there is no movement, no sound, no pouncing killer. There is just a quietly moaning animal getting blood and slobber all over my duffel bag.

Vince gets him on a leash. Bullets has trouble getting up.

"Maybe we should carry him," I say.

By way of response, he yanks the leash along, tells the dog, "Get moving." And it does. We all do.

We crunch through packed snow whiskered by the stems of skinny fierce-willed brush, and long wooden stakes tasseled by neon orange strips flapping in the wind like headbands. We would make believe they were broadswords and would sword-fight and drive them into the earth like Excalibur when one of us won, back when we used to roam around these hills, this forest, pretending it was all ours and would be for all time.

In one hand, Vince has the leash. In the other, he's got the hacksaw, dangling from the pinkie of his bad hand.

The moon glows, eviscerating a wad of clouds as we enter the woods. An old tree stump is just up ahead, in a clearing atop a gentle rise. I think the dog is lucky, in a way. Such a beautiful place. As if it can read my thoughts it thrashes against the leash, refusing to be led, flicking blood in its tirade.

"Get a rock or something will you?" Vince says. "Damn dog is stubborn."

There aren't any rocks in sight. But there is a good size log.

"Tie off the leash on that trunk," he says, handing it to me. "Then we'll stun him. Set him up on the stump."

I trudge off to the oak he pointed at, and, looping the leash around it, make a kind of pulley I can crank the dog back with.

"Remember when we used to pretend we were Arctic explorers, Vince?"

"I don't have time for memory lane here, Ant. Hit the dog and let's go." He draws a hipper of Canadian Club from his jacket pocket and pulls from it hard and tosses the bottle to me. "Go on."

When I move toward Bullets, he maintains distance.

"We're not playin' that game, Ant," Vince says. "I got to come at him from the other side, or you'll be chasing him all fucking night." He sighs and swears in the dark, annoyed this is all more tricky than he imagined.

"Go slow," I call to him, "and go kind of in a roundabout way, so he doesn't catch on what you're up to."

"I know how to do it."

Vince hikes off. Bullets and I take stock of each other. He hasn't really been that real until now. I take a seat in the snow. "Hi again," I whisper.

"You know we could probably just do nothing and let this thing choke itself out," I call out to Vince.

He snorts at that.

Then I catch him snapping branches as he stalks up behind the tree where the dog's tied. Bullets hears too. He comes charging through the snow.

Vince backtracks in a panic, and Bullets winces when the end of the leash checks his advance. He scrambles to retreat. The fright in Vince's eyes would have been revenge enough almost, were I the dog, I think, as it lunges with fresh adrenaline against the leash. I approach from behind and though it is with heartfelt, advanced apology, I do crown the poor son of a bitch.

The dog's body becomes dead weight. Vince stomps up ahead of me.

"This is dumb."

"Let's move," he says, then takes the dog himself, who is already coming-to. With his good hand, he heaves it atop the tree stump. Mean-spirited, the wind thrashes and the drifts come alive like a disturbed nocturnal swarm fleeing the presence of some cloaked predator just beyond detection. The hacksaw's in the snow, a few feet away.

As he reaches for it with his bad hand, even I can see how painful it is—his fingers tremble; Vince is sweating, and that is when, after making sure that log's one wicked knot is face-down like the stud of a mace, and with all what strength I am able to summon, I bring it down.

I had closed my eyes. There is only whimpering.

I open them to find him face down in the snow, toiling to right himself. It's almost peaceful again, but it doesn't last. Vince is rolling around, too injured to breathe at first. He cradles his hand, moaning and wriggling around. It gives me the shivers.

"*You broke it,*" he grunts, "*it's broke, ah…*"

I have the leash half undone by then, unlooping it 'round the tree like a jackass to get it free. Telling the dog it dare not fuss now, but the dog's already drained, the adrenaline burned off. I have to haul him in a kind of bear hug, all the way back, down the hill, through the pretty woods, the dead field, past the chain and the sign, back to the Cutlass. And the snow comes down so dense I almost wonder whether there are brats in the trees emptying feather pillows above us.

I open the back door and buckle him in, looking Bullets in the face for the first time in years. His mouth is a mess of broken teeth and bloody sockets. I can't imagine him living long. His eyes are swimming.

I search my pockets, and when I find it, I put the leftover half pill of oxy in my palm. Bullets looks at me, looks at it, looks at me. I crush it up as good as I can, then swipe his tongue with the crumble, and smear his nose with the powder that's left. He doesn't like it, gives a kind of sneeze, but I think some made it down.

Then I remember—I don't have the damn keys.

*

Both Vince and I've seen enough movies to know that what's waiting for me at the top of the rise is nothing I will ever expect.

He could be anywhere by now. Behind a tree. Holed up in some barn or shed nearby. For all I know Vince buried himself in the snow and is waiting for me. Wouldn't put it past him.

When the wind pauses in its tantrums, the lumpy flakes of snow fall thick as ticker tape. It is bewitching and also suddenly suspect, as though some diversion or manner of sorcery Vince somehow managed to conjure. I step lightly and need another weapon.

But, when I spot his form, he is sitting on the tree stump. I get nearer and see him crying, shivering, staring at the useless hands in his lap like he's reading an invisible book.

"Give me the keys," I say. "Just give me the keys and I'll take you back and we can drop the dog off with the cops or something."

"You're a real disgrace to your family, you know. And to us. Fuck away from me, go back wherever."

I take a knee in front of him. "Let me have the keys, man. Come on. We are too old to be doing this."

Vince kicks me in the jaw. I don't recall ever being kicked in the jaw before. Great thud like hitting water off the high dive. Clutch of blackout moments where who knows.

There's a little slide in the snow. After I'm laid out, down the rise a bit. Hearing laugher hiss past teeth. When I gain my feet, he falls apart, cackling at me, my half-snowed face.

"There," he laughs, "now we're even, you spooky fucking queer."

I rush him, start to strangle him. He gurgles it again, "We're even, you—funging—ng."

I let up.

"We're even," he repeats, gulping air. "In my inner pocket."

Shaking my head, I search his coat and in that pocket, there's the bottle of pills.

"Gimme a couple," he says.

"I should wring your damn neck, Vince, give me the *keys*."

"I'll *give* you the keys. Do the pills first."

Popping the cap, I let two drop onto his tongue, which he sticks out like he's catching snowflakes. And he does catch a few, inadvertently. Then I pop one for myself. A whole one this time.

"Where's that whisky at?"

I search around us, spot it by where the dog was tied, and take a gulp and hold it out to Vince. He takes it from me, gently, with his left, less-bad hand.

"Outer left pocket," he says.

And there's where the keys are, which I take, and then sit down in the snow again for a minute, glad that's all over. Vince tries using his forearms to drink from the bottle again. Looks like a trained sea lion.

We give ourselves a minute. Uneasy peace between us, disquiet we'll forget hopefully soon enough, as we count on the substances to do the work. Just sit there breathing.

"They help with the cold," he says, like an expert.

I nod, punch drunk.

"You know," I say, "this has all gotten so boring." Even the storm falls into a sort of lull that suggests it too could use a break.

I give a great dazed yawn, and with nothing else to add, we hold out for the warmth to course before making any moves, and watch the clouds begin to congeal over a pristine lake of night. Pure, viscous darkness. Almost syrup.

I wake on the forest floor, to flurries burying me. For a moment, I make no move at all. *This is how it must feel,* I think to myself. Vince is vanished, as far as I can tell. I've never had much idea where he goes, when he disappears, never much cared. I'm dead-legged getting back to the car. Bullets is still in the back, panting frost and clawing up the windowpane once I'm in sight.

I thank the Lord of Duralast when that engine whinnies and turns.

It's one of those dead-end lanes like a runway to nowhere. I back up, make a three-point turnaround. As I'm heading off toward 94, I see a form rise from that potholed square of bare, buckled asphalt where the Cutlass had been. There he is. Like he just got out of bed.

I think: Vincent Von Jovic: the one who dares crawl underneath cars, where it's maybe warmest in a blizzard. Who, when he sees me driving off, in his own vehicle, instead of doing anything else, of all things, decides to wave. I thought that was his sum total, but I figured wrong. I'm always wrong, thank god. He looks like a stranger out there, waving at me like I'm some passing frigate and he's ashore with nothing better to do. Doesn't flag me down, chuck a rock, run after the car—he waves bye bye.

And he doesn't deserve it, and I don't know if he can even see, but still, I wave back.

*

The AM radio weatherman calls it a symptom of the polar vortex, the blizzard that is shredding its way northwest. He says all airports are shuttered, that the freeways are suicide in every direction except due south-southeast.

I-55 isn't a death trap yet, though the lines dividing the lanes are sketchier with each glance. I follow in the wake of a Maersk 18-wheeler. If this is smart or unwise, as a tactic, is irrelevant. It's the only one.

Keeping my eyes open is a task. My lids feel weighted. Bullets, quiet in back. If I can just make it out of this state. Think I might dodge the worst of this, keeping to the middle of what I guess is the middle of the lane as best I can, since the car responds to any turn of the wheel on a lag that gets longer and longer, until at some point it won't respond at all and we'll start sliding.

The radio says Indiana is getting clobbered, but it's not getting shellacked like here, not yet. If this setup lasts—if the Maersk and me can keep this up, can keep it nice and steady—we could be home before noon tomorrow. By sunset, surely.

It is as I'm thinking this that the Maersk lights up quadruple red ahead of me, starts to snake, then hydroplane, its wheels spinning and churning powder like a steamboat's impeller as it jackknifes across all four lanes while I'm slamming the brakes, which makes us go pinwheeling down the lane.

Our tandem skid slows to a stop, and by then we've both pulled about a one-eighty, and Bullets is awake. A minivan behind us honks and slows. I flash my high beams. In the rearview, I watch it reversing. When it's up beside me, the window on the passenger side rolls down. I roll down mine.

"Get. Off. The *road*!" yells the driver.

I just nod extra big and bring my window up. Not about to have a dialogue. Of the twelve odd Pall Mall cigarette packs lying throughout the car, not one of them has an actual square inside it. Vince's car's stupid wiper blades wag their fingers in my face, all of which, taken together, I take as sign to maybe stop driving.

The next exit takes a half-century to get to. Slicks of black ice make the ramp a real joy, and that kind of dry-mashed snow that sticks to tire tread is not helpful. But if we don't maintain speed we run the risk of slipping into the sidewinding drifts that the winds are lashing across the plains hard enough they seem to sandblast them into sharp objects. The cross winds nearly turn us like a dial, but we make it down.

Hanging a left puts it at our backs. I don't even really need to press the accelerator. We cruise toward the lights of whatever village this is, and when we pull into the lot of the first motel we come across, it does not feel at all corny or blasphemous to cross myself and praise those gales that delivered us.

*

"I need a room, man."

The kid at the counter clucks and wags his head, flipping through the ledger on his desk. "I'm afraid we don't have any vacancies, sir. Full house cuz of the storm."

"It's an emergency. I'll take whatever you got. I'll take a broom closet."

The kid has such a good-natured chuckle. Thinks I'm joshing. "Sir, I'm sorry. There's nothing I can do. I'm just working the desk tonight."

"Have you been outside lately?"

"Uh… no, sir. I have a good view though. Super Jack London out there."

He doesn't understand. I need to make him comprehend.

"I know you're just doing your job. You're following orders here—I get that. I've got an injured dog. You like dogs? I'm on like four hours sleep over the past forty-eight. I'm begging here.

Anything, a couch, a broom closet, a fucking sock drawer. Just a few hours. You don't know what kind of day I've had."

The kid pauses, thinking, chewing his lip. Flipping through his ledger. I'm burning a hole through his forehead with my glare. "I just—we have a phone you can use? You can maybe call around? I don't know there's anything I can do, sir, you should've... I'd ask my manager but—"

"Look, what if my wife was pregnant out there in that car?"

"I-I'd say go to the... hospital...?"

"Where's the fucking phone."

The kid points down the hall.

"Tell me your name."

"Tim?"

"I expected more from you, Tim. I am disappointed."

"I am sorry for your predicament, sir. People from around here, they know better than to travel in these conditions. Rooms go fast. It's not your fault."

"Thanks, Tim. That's good to know."

I call Caroline and let her know her better half is out there like a buffoon in the storm and that she might want to think about searching for him. She tells me that he's already home, though. That he's been home for a while now. They're getting ready to have some chili.

"Wow. Okay... good to hear."

"And since we're on the subject what the hell happened to Vince's hand? Ant? Care to answer? Where *are* you? And where in the *world* is our *car*?"

Before I can explain she says, "Know what—forget it, I'll ask him and we'll deal with it. Ant, do us all a favor?"

"Anything."

"Don't come back."

She hangs up.

There is a soda machine beside the ice machine in the hallway off the lobby. I feed it a five, get a few water bottles, a couple Cherry Cokes, zip up my jacket, and head back out in the storm to the car.

*

He had vomited at some point while I was dealing with Tim. First thing I do is wash his face. I do so carefully, dabbing at him with a wad of bottled water-drenched napkins I found in the glove box. His muzzle, his throat are swollen, the injuries still so fresh I am afraid that if he moves too much he'll start bleeding again. He's already lost so much. I'm doing what I can. He only has one unbroken tooth left, his left lower canine. He is feverish to the touch and shuddering. Attacking us would have hurt him ten times worse than anything he could have done to us.

Soggy and pink, the napkins go splat on the floor in back.

"I missed the funeral, missed my flight, almost killed you, and that jerkoff beat me home," I say to the dog, and lower the seat down by him to stroke his ear.

I turn the engine on to get some heat going, hit the overhead lights. Or, I think, should I be packing him with snow?

"Gonna get you to a vet. Don't worry, bud." Outside a plow shovels past, its lone yellow misery light spinning, all heavy scrape and salt spray.

I massage the muscular base of his neck. Bullets looks around.

"Not sure what to do, bud," I tell him. His ribs wheeze up and down in shallow swells like a squeeze box. "You'd think I would know."

He seems scared. Like he's waiting for a vaccination. The wind has the Cutlass going side to side.

My nose at his ear, I whisper that he is not allowed to go.
I realize then—I am terrified.

"How about let's be friends. How that sound? Let bygones be
bygones. Blink once if you're with me.

"You have to stay though, bud. You have to stay right here.
That's the deal. Stupid storm's scaring you. Be gone in a bit. And
we'll get you fixed up, we'll get you squared away. We'll get you
a new grill. All chrome? That sound good?"

I tell him: "Stay." I am sick of this. Not another one.

"Just you have to hang a little while more. That a deal?"

I smooth his white coat. I can't see anything clear at all now,
but there's no need really. Lowering my forehead to his, smelling
his fur, I whisper: "I'm sorry. Okay? I am sorry. Truce?"

Because I outlived everyone I love, and now there is nothing left except this one last raw, shredded nerve that is singing
through me now, singing a pain I thought was lost to me but
is here and now and singing right through me. I feel it. It's all
I feel, I am alive with it. It's all right now. So I hold on, and I let
it sing, and despite the fact it cannot change anything, that in all
likelihood it means nothing, and even if he knows I of all people
can't deliver, Bullets gives me a paw, drapes it over my forearm.
I stroke the valley between his eyes with my thumb. We make
a little pact, a covenant, just between us strays. We shake on it.

Two Dollar Radio
Books too loud to Ignore

ALSO AVAILABLE
Here are some other titles you might want to dig into.

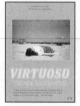

VIRTUOSO NOVEL BY YELENA MOSKOVICH

← "A bold feminist novel." —*Times Literary Supplement*

← "Told through multiple unique, compelling voices, the book's time and action are layered, with possibilities and paths forming rhythmic, syncopated interludes that emphasize that history is now."
— Letitia Montgomery-Rodgers, *Foreword Reviews, starred review*

WITH A DISTINCTIVE PROSE FLAIR and spellbinding vision, a story of love, loss, and self-discovery that heralds Yelena Moskovich as a brilliant and one-of-a-kind visionary.

SOME OF US ARE VERY HUNGRY NOW
ESSAYS BY ANDRE PERRY

← "A complete, deep, satisfying read." —Gabino Iglesias, NPR

ANDRE PERRY'S DEBUT COLLECTION of personal essays travels from Washington DC to Iowa City to Hong Kong in search of both individual and national identity while displaying tenderness and a disarming honesty.

SAVAGE GODS MEMOIR BY PAUL KINGSNORTH

← "Like all the best books, [*Savage Gods* is] a wail sent up from the heart of one of the intractable problems of the human condition: real change comes only from crisis, and crisis always involves loss... There are few writers as raw or brave on the page. Savage Gods is an important book."
—Ellie Robins, *Los Angeles Review of Books*

SAVAGE GODS ASKS, can words ever paint the truth of the world—or are they part of the great lie which is killing it?

THE BOOK OF X NOVEL BY SARAH ROSE ETTER

→ A Best Book of 2019 —*Vulture*

← "Etter brilliantly, viciously lays bare what it means to be a woman in the world, what it means to hurt, to need, to want, so much it consumes everything." —Roxane Gay

A SURREAL EXPLORATION OF ONE WOMAN'S LIFE and death against a landscape of meat, office desks, and bad men.

TRIANGULUM NOVEL BY MASANDE NTSHANGA

← "Magnificently disorienting and meticulously constructed, *Triangulum* couples an urgent subtext with an unceasing sense of mystery. This is a thought-provoking dream of a novel, situated within thought-provoking contexts both fictional and historical." —Tobias Carroll, Tor.com

AN AMBITIOUS, OFTEN PHILOSOPHICAL AND GENRE-BENDING NOVEL that covers a period of over 40 years in South Africa's recent past and near future.